EXPOSE ME

KAYDENCE SNOW

Expose Me

By Kaydence Snow

Published by Sonder Publishing Pty Ltd Copyright © 2022 Kaydence Snow

Immortal Vices and Virtues universe Copyright © 2022 Kel Carpenter LLC.

Edited by: Melinda Andrews

Cover design by Yocla Designs

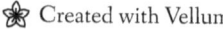 Created with Vellum

CHAPTER 1

As the bartender slid my drink over, the petite vampire at the dark end of the bar slid her teeth into her date's neck. Even in heels, she had to stretch to reach him, but he held her close and hunched down as she drank.

These things usually took place in private, but this fine establishment was in No Man's Land, and no one cared. They were being more discreet than the couples sloppily grinding on each other on the dance floor. I took a sip of my French martini and scanned the space casually. No one had come in since I'd ordered. My client was late.

I was giving him until I reached the bottom of my glass before I left. Despite the less than stellar setting, the cocktail was actually pretty good. It would be a shame to waste it.

The bar was just off a main street in the north of Melbourne—not hidden away enough to only attract regulars, but not so busy that it was hard to keep an eye on the door. Perfect for conducting business.

The door opened, but I was distracted from seeing who

came through it by the inebriated human who sidled up next to me, leaning way too heavily on the bar.

"Hey there—"

"No." I cut off his slurring and sipped my drink. Thankfully—for him—he decided I was more effort than I was worth, and he stumbled away just as a man in a suit made his way through the crowd.

We'd never met, but I was the only one in the place with magenta hair. Not exactly hard to miss.

He wasn't hard to miss either. He was the only one in a suit and tie when everyone else was in some combination of denim and leather.

I slid off my barstool, drink in hand, and stood straight as he reached me.

"Uh, hi, are you Jen?" he asked, looking a bit nervous. Jen wasn't my real name. What I was doing wasn't exactly forbidden, but my regular employer wouldn't take kindly to knowing I was doing it on the side.

"Who wants to know?" I asked, watching him over the rim of my glass.

"I'm Robbie. We spoke on the phone about . . ." he trailed off as he glanced around.

"Let's talk over here." I turned and led the way to a small table on the opposite side of the room to the dance floor. The two tub chairs put our backs to the wall as we sat.

"So, how's your evening?" Robbie asked, crossing his legs, then uncrossing them. "Can I get you a—"

"Do you have the photos?" I cut him off, holding my hand out. He leaned back in his seat and reached into the inside pocket of his suit jacket.

"Right to business then. OK. Good," he muttered to himself as he pulled out two photos.

I took them and studied the first one. It was very old and

featured a young woman with an updo and wearing an old-fashioned dress. I didn't pay much attention to her features, focusing instead on the necklace she wore.

"That's my great grandmother," Robbie supplied unhelpfully and started babbling about the history of his family. I tuned him out and looked at the second photo. Another woman, with similar features to the first, was pictured next to a man that looked a bit like Robbie. It was a wedding photo, and she wore the same necklace.

Robbie had moved on to telling me how the necklace had been passed down and worn by his mother on her wedding day, and *blah blah blah*. I studied the jewelry in the two images. The necklace was platinum, twenty diamonds set into it—ten on either side of the brilliant teardrop sapphire at the center.

"How long ago was it stolen?" I asked, cutting off whatever he'd been babbling about.

"Uh, maybe six months ago now," he said. "The investigator from my House couldn't find any leads, and I'm pretty sure they've given up now. It was taken right out of my parents' home. Lucky they weren't there! They took a few other things too, but this is the one that's really valuable. Not to mention that it has huge sentimental value for my family."

"Yes, you said as much on the phone." I nodded. He was repeating everything he'd already told me. I hated wasting time, and he was getting on my nerves. "And as I said, I require payment up front."

"So, you can find it then?" His eyes lit up.

I narrowed my own. "Like I said, I make no guarantees." Again—all things we'd already discussed. "But I have enough to look."

For once, he kept his mouth shut and reached into his

pants pocket. He pulled out a pouch and placed it on the table between us, the contents clinking together. At least he could follow instructions. I tucked the pouch—containing three vials of shifter blood—into my coat pocket and leaned back in the chair.

With one last look at the photos, I closed my eyes and searched.

Had I held the necklace previously, remembered what its weight felt like in my hand, what its energy was like, I could've summoned it—made it appear in my grip. I had to have touched an item to be able to summon it, or one identical to it. I mean, all bananas were pretty much the same—energetically speaking. Same with mass-produced things. But unique or personal items that someone had emotional attachment to were a whole other ballgame.

As it was, all I had to go off were the pictures. The old one proved his family's ownership; I didn't use my power to steal, much as others wished I did, or *suspected* I did. The newer image strengthened the proof of ownership and confirmed the client's connection to the item. It would've been easier if I'd been able to meet with the mother—her connection to the necklace was stronger as she'd worn it, owned it. But he'd refused. Didn't want to get her hopes up. Whatever. My fee was the same regardless.

Holding on to the photos, I tuned in to the energy of the necklace. It was faint, barely a lead to follow.

I cracked my eyes open and held my hand out, palm up. "Take my hand."

Robbie rubbed his hands on his thighs and gently placed his clammy hand in mine. I closed my eyes again and gripped his fingers firmly.

The extra connection helped, and I started to see them —tendrils of energy. Like ribbons floating on the breeze, wisps of energy beckoned me to follow them. I grabbed on to the strongest one and tugged, then checked out a few of the others. They all led to different locations.

I sighed and dropped Robbie's hand before opening my eyes. He stared at me intently, his eyes wide with hope.

I downed the rest of my cocktail and carefully placed the glass back on the table.

"Well? Did you find it?" he couldn't help asking, the suspense clearly killing him.

"I'm sorry." I squared my shoulders and shook my head. He frowned, his gaze flicking to the pocket where I'd tucked away his payment. He was a shifter of some kind, but I wasn't sure what. Shifters tended to underestimate me. He could try to take it back, some unsatisfied clients did, but he'd just end up on his ass and bruised. I was up-front about my terms.

"The item no longer exists," I explained, hoping to defuse the situation.

"What?" He frowned.

"Whoever stole it has taken it apart and sold the precious stones separately. I could tell you which general area they're all in, but they're all over the place, and there's no way to identify the specific gems that came from that necklace." I got to my feet, keeping my arms loose, ready to grab the blade at my thigh if necessary. "I'd let it go and move on if I were you. It's gone."

He slumped in his chair, and I turned around and made my way through the crowd. I'd told him all there was to know and had nothing left to say. Our business was done.

At the door I checked to make sure he wasn't being stupid and following me, but he'd gone to the bar, to drown his disappointment, no doubt.

❧ ❧ ❧

I pulled my satin trench coat closer around my body, but I didn't duck my head against the wind. It was not smart to lose focus of your surroundings. The urge was strong though. It had been warm, balmy even, when I headed out for dinner earlier that night. But in true Melbourne fashion, the weather had turned in a matter of minutes, and it was cold now, the wind carrying a sharp bite.

It was just one more block to the building where I was staying, and just three more days until my official business here was done. The House of Spirit and Sapphire was expanding its territory in Melbourne, and I'd been tasked with overseeing the changes. Our headquarters was in Sydney, and that's where I lived—when I wasn't traveling on House business, which was often. Odin and Lady Gabriella, the elected leaders of our House, were based there, as were most of the high-ranking members.

There had been seven Houses—established after the portal in Portland opened and exposed the supernatural species that had been living among humans in secret for hundreds of years. After the discovery of a new species of phantom in Scotland a few months back, a new House had been established, so now there were eight. Eight Houses holding territories all over the world and leaving the spaces between lawless, dangerous No Man's Land.

A lot of Spirit and Sapphire members had been settling in Melbourne over the past few years, so it was time to expand our territory.

We had a base of operations in what used to be the parliament building. I'd spent nearly two weeks in endless meetings there, but I was staying in an apartment building owned by Spirit and Sapphire several blocks away.

I turned down the side street. It was empty. Up ahead, light from the lobby of my building spilled onto the street. I picked up my pace, ready to get inside and into a warm bed.

As I passed a narrow alleyway that ran between two buildings, something in the darkness moved. I had my dagger in the palm of my hand faster than you could blink, my body poised for action, my senses on alert. The sound was a kind of shuffling, like a cardboard box scraping against brick. Maybe a homeless person? I guessed it was possible they had snuck past House guards and into our territory. But then came a metallic thud, followed by a low, pained moan.

My eyes were adjusting to the heavy darkness, and I could just make out the corner of a dumpster. Was someone getting beaten up behind there? I knew my superiors wouldn't want me to get involved, that I should just contact some guards to deal with it, but I hesitated. They wouldn't want me running my side hustle either, so whatever.

"Hey, you alright in there?" I called, not too loudly, but with a firm, level voice.

After a beat of silence, the shuffling sound came again, and a figure emerged from the darkness, leaning heavily on the dumpster.

The woman was petite, her long blonde hair obscuring her face. She was completely nude.

"He . . . hey . . ." she mumbled, and she sounded winded. She was hunched over, gripping her middle.

Ice ran through my veins, and I scanned the darkness again.

"Are you alone?" I asked, taking careful steps towards her. "Are they still here?"

"Al . . . alone . . ." came the weak reply. I believed her. If this was some kind of trap, they would've made a move already. This poor woman had clearly been attacked, possibly raped, and left nude to rot in a dirty alleyway. In *our* territory—where all members of the House of Spirit and Sapphire were supposed to be safe. I kind of *wished* whoever had done this was still around.

I tucked my murderous rage away along with my dagger and gently grabbed the woman's shoulder. She flinched, but a quick scan of her body didn't show any bruises or cuts. I frowned, confused. She was actually remarkably clean—like she'd just taken all her clothes off moments before stumbling towards me.

Maybe the bruises just weren't showing yet. There was no denying she was hurt. Her body trembled slightly under my touch, and her face was screwed up in pain.

"You're safe now," I told her in a gentle tone. "I'm going to call the House guards, OK?"

She shook her head. "No. No authori . . . ty."

"A healer then." I reached for my phone in my back pocket, but her hand shot out with surprising speed and gripped my wrist. Her grip was weak, but her intentions were clear.

"No." She fixed me with a firm look before her face screwed up in pain again. "Water."

I sighed and took my coat off, draping the fabric over her shoulders and helping her maneuver her arms into it.

"Water," she said again, looking like she might collapse onto the ground at any moment.

It was fucking freezing out here, and she didn't even have shoes on. Even if I ignored her request, I couldn't make her stand out in the cold and wait for the authorities.

"OK, come on, let's get you warm." I wrapped an arm around her waist and lifted her arm around my neck. She leaned against me heavily and stumbled along as I slowly walked us to the brightly lit lobby.

"Water," she murmured again.

"Yes, I'll get you some water," I reassured her. "We have to go in here to get it. I'll take you to my apartment, and you can have all the water you want."

There was no response, and she slumped further against me. I was taking most of her weight as we crossed the shiny tiled floor to the elevators. I pressed the button and readjusted my grip on the woman.

It took a bit of maneuvering to get my keycard out of my pocket without dropping the injured woman, but I managed it, and we reached the eighteenth floor without any stops. It was late—no one else was around.

By the time we made it up the hall and to my door, her feet were dragging on the carpet. I swiped my card, kicked the door open, and leaned down to pick her up. I was practically carrying her anyway, and she was so slight, she barely weighed anything.

I deposited her on the couch and poured a big glass of water. She was so weak she needed me to help her hold it, but once the water hit her lips, she tipped the glass up and chugged it all in about four gulps.

"Water," she said, licking the drops off her lips.

"You want more?" I raised my brows.

"More water. Please."

"OK." I shrugged and filled up a jug instead, bringing that over with a full glass.

She chugged the second one down just as fast and reached for the jug. Her hands were shaky, but she was strong enough to lift it and pour.

"I'm going to get you something to wear and then we can talk about calling a healer to check you over," I said, heading for the bedroom. There was no response, so I prepared myself for an argument as I grabbed a pair of sweats and a T-shirt.

I was only gone for the few minutes it took me to put on something warmer and grab clothes for the naked woman, but I came back to the living room to find her collapsed awkwardly against the back of the couch.

"Shit." I rushed to her side and checked her pulse, releasing a relieved breath when I found it was normal. Her mouth was open, and she was snoring softly on every other breath, so at least she wasn't dying. My prodding hadn't roused her, so I put what first aid I knew to use and checked for broken bones or bleeding, or anything that would be life-threatening.

There wasn't a thing wrong with her. I sat back on my heels and frowned. Was this some kind of overdose? It didn't look like the result of any human-made substances, but the fae and the witches were constantly coming up with new ways for people to get high.

I considered calling a healer anyway, but she seemed fine, and she really didn't want the authorities involved. Maybe this was a domestic violence situation? In the end, I decided to let her sleep it off. If she was faking it and waiting for me to fall asleep so she could rob me, she'd be sorely disappointed. I kept my most prized possessions in a place no one but me could reach, and I slept with a blade under my pillow. No one had gotten the jump on me in a very long time.

I gently lowered her head to a cushion and lifted her feet off the ground before covering her with a blanket. When I placed the spare clothes on the coffee table, I spotted the jug and glass. Both were drained.

This small woman got more and more curious. How the

hell did she drink that much water in a few minutes, and where did it go? Her stomach was tiny.

Whatever. I was too tired to deal with this. I filled the jug again and left it next to her before heading to bed. If she was still there in the morning, I'd try to speak to her, get her some help if I could.

What I found on my couch the next morning made me wish I'd kept walking past that alleyway.

CHAPTER 2

I slept undisturbed. The petite blonde didn't try to kill me or rob me, and I didn't hear the front door, so I guessed she was still on my couch. Shit, I hoped she wasn't dead.

The thought had me ignoring my full bladder and heading straight for the living room in my sleep shorts and tank.

Nothing in the apartment looked disturbed, but the woman was no longer on the couch. In her place was a . . . I couldn't say it was a man exactly, but the figure was twice her size and curled up in the same position I'd left her in.

I swallowed down the sound of shock that tried to claw its way up my throat and kept very still. With little more than a thought, I summoned a handgun from my secure storage facility. The weight of the weapon was comforting in my hands, but I had no idea if it would do anything against the creature.

Had it consumed the young woman? How had it even gotten into the apartment?

It was wearing my satin trench coat. The fabric was ripped at the seams and barely hanging on—like a scene from *The Hulk*. The woman had been swimming in it. But she wasn't a woman; she wasn't even human. She was this creature all along.

What species was this? I didn't know of any vampire, fae, witch, or god who looked like this.

It was humanoid in shape—it had a torso, legs, arms, a head—but that's where the similarities ended. It was black, *pitch-black*. The sun was shining brightly through the windows, bathing the whole room in light, which fell directly on the creature on the couch. But it was not reflecting off its skin like it would any other creature. There was no visual difference between the parts of it in sunlight and in shade. It was like it absorbed the light itself.

And that wasn't even the most disturbing part.

It had no face.

There was a head attached to shoulders, but where there should've been eyes, a nose, a mouth, or even some kind of bone structure, there was nothing but more smooth, black surface.

Was this a new species to Earth? The latest new portal opened in Portland about fifty years ago, and the one before that appeared hundreds of years before. It wasn't exactly a common occurrence.

The Houses would know if there was a new portal. Word would've spread. Unless it had *just* happened.

Holy shit! I'd made first contact with a new species. I needed to find out where the portal was. I needed to call this in. I needed to find out if they were friendly or intending to wage war.

A horrible thought struck me then, and the gun shook in

my hand just a bit. The woman had been hurt in some way, practically passing out in my arms. And now she was a disturbing new creature on my couch. Whatever they were, they could shapeshift. What if they'd been here for longer than anyone knew, blending in with us, waging a secret war.

"Fuck," I breathed, unable to hold back the curse.

The thing on the couch woke up. It had no eyes to open, but it angled its head like it was looking at me, then slowly sat up.

It had fingers that dug into the couch cushions, and there was something different about its head. It was almost like soft pinpricks of light were shining from inside. No, not *from* inside—just inside. It was like looking into a glass ball with little lights pointing into the center. But the light was soft and swallowed up by the depthless black, so it was hard to tell.

"Water. Please."

It had no mouth to speak with, but I heard it loud and clear, speaking in a soft, androgenous voice. The pitcher and glass on the coffee table were empty.

"What are you?" I demanded, forcing steel into my voice.

It stared back at me for a moment, then started to shrink in on itself. Before my eyes, the strange creature morphed into the same petite blonde I'd helped the night before.

"I am weak and unable to hold my form while sleeping. Water will help," it said with the woman's mouth.

"What are you?" I gritted out again. "Which realm are you from? Start answering questions or I start shooting."

"I will not harm you," she—it—said.

"Oh, phew! Thanks for clarifying. I'll just make us a cup of tea, and everything can be peachy fucking keen."

"I would prefer the water plain, rather than filtered through tea leaves."

I blinked at her—it was hard to think of her as an *it* when the fragile, vulnerable woman from last night sat before me. "Do you not understand sarcasm?" I kept my gun steady.

"No." She tilted her head to the side. "Ah, now I do. You were mocking me."

"No shit," I mumbled, frowning. There had to be a new portal somewhere. *Had to be.* This creature was way too clueless about everything.

The slight woman got to her feet. I stood my ground.

"What are you doing?" I barked. "Stay where you are."

"I can't." She shrugged, the torn-up sleeve of my trench coat slipping halfway down her arm. "If you will not bring me water, I must find it myself."

"Yeah? Well, if you don't sit your ass down and start answering questions, I must shoot you." I pointed to the couch with my gun.

"You would be wasting your ammunition. I cannot be hurt by projectile weapons." After a beat of silence, the first sign of any emotion other than pain, which was evident in her every movement, showed on her face—irritation. "Yes, I am from a realm you would be unfamiliar with. I can explain everything, but I really do need water first."

I hesitated. She was clearly an intelligent life-form, probably more advanced than humans—or what was left of us. We'd evolved so much with all the magic coursing through the planet, it was hard to say what *human* even meant anymore. And she was definitely not in a good way last night and hadn't tried to kill me while I slept.

"Fine. There's the kitchen sink. Have all the water you

want. But I'm keeping my gun pointed." I wasn't just going to take her word for it that my weapon couldn't hurt her.

"There is more water behind that wall." She pointed to the bathroom and casually walked towards me. Stubborn little . . . I sighed. Whatever. I could keep an eye on her just as easily in the shower as I could at the sink.

I backed out of her path, keeping my gun trained on her the entire time as I followed her into the bathroom.

She cranked the water to full blast, dropped my tattered coat to the floor, and stepped under the spray.

She didn't adjust the temperature, letting the water sluice over her body cold. I guessed there'd been no need to worry about her freezing last night.

I resisted the urge to avert my gaze and give her privacy. I felt like a perv watching her shower, but the weight of the gun in my hand reminded me why I was being ridiculous.

Her skin rippled, reminding me further that I wasn't creepily watching a woman shower. She tipped her head back and opened her mouth directly under the spray as another round of ripples washed over her. Every time it happened, her true skin shimmered in the wake of the ripples, the depthless black showing for a split second.

Barely a trickle of water was going down the drain; most of it was going into her mouth and . . . being absorbed by her skin?

After a while, she shut the water off and turned to face me. Again, I resisted the urge to avert my gaze. Her tits were amazing and didn't even look fake. I wasn't sure whether to be jealous or aroused.

By the time she stepped out of the shower, she was prac-tically dry. Even her hair was sapped of all its moisture, the droplets disappearing before my eyes.

"Lower your weapon," she demanded in a soft voice, "we do not have time for this."

"Fuck you," I replied in just as soft a voice. "And there is no *we*."

Instead of replying, she moved faster than I'd ever seen anyone move and, for the first time in many years, my weapon was snatched out of my grip before I knew what was happening.

I dropped to the ground and twisted out of the bathroom. I'd dashed behind the kitchen counter and summoned another gun from my stash before I realized that I wasn't being shot at.

Heart hammering, I peeked over the counter.

She was standing at the door, looking right at me, her arms loose at her sides. I frowned as I slowly got to my feet and pointed my gun at her. Why wasn't she shooting?

Staring me in the eye, she slowly lifted the weapon. I tightened my grip on my own and prepared to fire but . . . she wasn't raising the gun to point at me. She had her arm bent, the gun pointing at an awkward angle. She lifted it to her head, barrel against the temple, and pulled the trigger.

My heart leapt into my throat. *What the fuck?* Dropping my gun on the counter, I darted to her side, but she wasn't falling to the floor.

There wasn't even any blood on the side of her head, let alone brains splattered all over the place. She stood in the same spot, looking at me as calmly as she had been a moment ago.

My phone went off, the special ringtone reserved for Reginald Reyes—my boss—cutting through the stunned silence. I ignored it, my full attention on trying to process what I'd just seen.

The petite blonde let the gun dangle from her finger by

the trigger guard and held it out to me. Numbly, I took it and looked at it to make sure it was indeed my gun—the one I knew was loaded with live rounds and had been cleaned just last month.

The woman lifted her hand up to her mouth and spat out the bullet.

"What the fuck," I breathed, still struggling to process what I was seeing.

"I cannot be hurt by projectile weapons," she repeated, her tone more firm and her expression more irritated.

"Yeah." I shook my head to clear some of the stupefied fog that had settled around it. "Yep, point made."

My survival instincts started to return, along with a heavy dose of curiosity. I caressed one of my most familiar threads in my mind and summoned my favorite blade. The Fairbairn Sykes fighting knife was one of the last things my mother had given me. I was fifteen, and she died a month later, leaving me all alone in a merciless world. It was all black—from the tip of the blade to the end of the handle—and had a sapphire embedded in the end of the handle.

I hadn't really decided I was going to stab her; I was just kind of curious and acting on reflex. But she took the decision out of my hands along with the knife and stabbed herself in the chest without even flinching.

"Holy—" I startled and snatched the knife back. "Would you stop that?" I admonished, watching in fascination as the wound closed within seconds, not a drop of blood in sight. All I saw at the gaping wound before it disappeared was that depthless black.

"I am not trying to harm you," she said, sounding exasperated. "It would be nice if you could show me the same courtesy."

To be fair, she was right. Didn't mean I was ready to

trust her—just because she hadn't tried to kill me yet didn't mean she wouldn't. But I didn't think I was in any immediate danger.

"Yeah, OK, fair enough." I sighed.

She nodded. "I need to know more about your ability to summon items. Is this something all inhabitants of this realm can do? How does it work?"

"Jeez, buy me dinner before you start getting into the personal shit," I scoffed.

She cocked her head to the side, some of that frustration showing in her frown. "This can't wait until after the evening meal."

"I . . ." I waved her off. Not worth it. "Never mind. At least put some clothes on. It's distracting."

She looked down at her body, then back at me and gave me a look like she didn't see the problem.

I pointed at the clothes I'd left for her the night before and left her to it to tend to my bladder, which was now screaming to be released. As I took a few minutes to do basic, normal things—like pee and put clothes on myself—my practical side returned. I needed to get in contact with the House of Spirit and Sapphire to report this. The portal would need to be secured and monitored.

"I have put the clothing on." The blonde appeared at the door to the bedroom. "Now tell me about your power. It is important."

"Why is it so important?" I frowned, grabbing my phone and moving past her to the kitchen. I needed something that was more than coffee but less than cocaine to deal with this situation. A very clever witch had come up with exactly this and sold it in potion form all over the world. Unfortunately, I had no VitaBrew in my apartment; coffee would have to do. I switched on the espresso machine—one of the best things about Melbourne was the exceptional coffee—and pushed the button for a latte. I had several cases of VitaBrew in my secure storage facility and made a mental note to summon one later. It was probably best to conserve my power, considering how unpredictable my day had been so far.

"I need to find something. Your ability would make that much easier," she said.

"What do you need to find?" I asked, watching the coffee trickle into the steamed milk. She was being kind of intense about this, and I had a feeling this was important information to get.

"Something of great importance," she said.

"Yeah, well, I can't find it if I don't even know what it is or what it looks like." I sighed and took a sip of coffee.

"Then take me to someone who can."

"I don't know anyone who can find something without more info than 'it's of great importance' so you're shit out of luck. There are witches who can do what I do, but even they need more details. Plus, they'll charge you a hefty price for it, and I'm pretty sure you didn't come here with any valuables."

Her frown deepened more and more as I spoke, clearly not happy with what I was saying.

"Anyway," I continued, "we're not going anywhere or doing anything until I call this in to the House of Spirit and Sapphire. And they're going to have a shitload of questions."

"Shitload?" She scrunched her face up. I chuckled, sipping more coffee. I couldn't help it. It was like talking to an alien. She had no idea about anything.

My phone started ringing again, that same distinctive tone. I'd already ignored Reginald once when I thought this bitch had blown her brains out in front of me. He did not like being ignored, and a glance at the time told me I should've left for work ten minutes ago.

"Well, this saves me one phone call at least," I mumbled, reaching for my cell.

The blonde darted forward and smacked it out of my hand, making me spill my coffee in the process.

"What the hell, dude?" I shoved her off me and wiped the precious spilled coffee off my arm with a tea towel.

"You cannot tell others I am here," she rushed out.

I rubbed my forehead. "I don't really have a choice. I have to report this. They're not going to hurt you. But you're in our territory and we have to—"

"There is no time!" She grabbed my forearm.

"Then you need to give me more information here. Look . . ." I extracted my arm from her grip. "What's your name?" I figured that was a good place to start. She just blinked at me, so I took a breath and forced myself not to get irritated. Maybe they didn't have names where she was from. "My name is Sky Serpell. That's what people call me when they're trying to get my attention or talking about me. What are you called?"

"My name is Zeymlardterrerdjormljerra," she said.

"OK, uh . . ." I tried to pronounce it like she had but gave up after the first three syllables, impressed that I'd managed even that much. "Sorry. Can you say it again?"

"You can call me Zey. It's what you call a nickname."

"Zey. OK great, I can work with that." I gave her a smile. "Now let's take a seat on the couch, I'll make myself another coffee and we can talk—"

"We have to leave," she cut me off, her eyes suddenly scanning the apartment, flying from the door to the windows.

"What?" I shook my head. "Calm down. Let's just—"

"It's not safe here. We must leave." Again with the cutting off.

"No." I crossed my arms and stood my ground. For a second, anyway. She grabbed me by the wrist and yanked me towards the door. Her grip was strong, bruising. I kicked the back of her knee and twisted out of it. She stumbled but didn't fall, managing to recover, twist, and lunge for me again.

I darted to the side and whacked her on the side of the head, but she still managed to grab my arm and twist it behind my back. Immediately she started yanking me towards the door. Now I was pissed. My first instinct was to summon a blade, but she'd already shown me that wouldn't do shit to her, so I settled into my hand-to-hand combat training.

Leaning forward as much as I could, I threw my weight back and pushed off with my feet hard. It threw us off balance, and her back smacked against the wall. I elbowed her in the stomach and wrenched my other arm free. Turning on the spot, I smacked her hands away as they reached for me and gripped her around the throat. I pinned one of her wrists to the wall next to her head and held tightly.

"You're a warrior." She flashed me something resembling a satisfied look, her voice perfectly fine even though I was squeezing her neck tightly enough to knock most people out. She seemed excited and was giving me the first smile I'd seen on her. Weirdo.

Behind me, glass shattered, the sound loud and intrusive in the small apartment. I whipped my head around to see the living room window smashed and a shape stepping through it.

The creature was pitch-black and faceless, and another two just like it were right behind the first.

"Friends of yours?" I cocked an eyebrow at Zey. Judging by the murderous look on her face and the fact they'd chosen to bust through the window, I was pretty sure they were more foe than friend.

CHAPTER 3

Instead of answering, Zey moved. In the blink of an eye, she turned us so it was now my back against the wall. I didn't stay there long. Zey wrenched the door open and shuffled me towards it. This time, I didn't fight her. The things coming through my window did not have a friendly vibe, as evidenced by the weird-looking thing one of them threw at us.

Zey stepped to the side and took the blow. I summoned three throwing knives in succession and threw them at our attackers. One by one, the blades embedded themselves in faceless heads.

"That won't stop them." Zey groaned, clutching her shoulder as the door swung closed.

"I know," I gritted out. Hopefully it would slow them down.

I gripped her around the waist, and we jogged up the hallway as fast as we could. I could've just left her there to deal with her own mess. She'd been nothing but a giant pain in my ass anyway. But she'd tried to protect me by getting me to leave before they got there, and then she'd taken a knife—or whatever it was—for me. Three on one wasn't a fair fight.

"Remove . . . the weapon." She winced in pain, trying and failing to reach it herself. It was buried in the back of her shoulder, and her skin was doing that weird ripple thing I'd seen in the shower. Only this time, the waves of smooth black were jagged and coming from the wound.

We rounded the corner, and I tuned in to the sound of a door opening and closing as I took a few precious seconds to grip the handle of the strange weapon and yank it out. Zey winced but didn't make a sound.

Hyperaware of the sound of approaching footsteps, I pocketed the weird five-pronged weapon and rushed towards the elevators. The footsteps were not slow, but not running either—a steady clip. Like they knew they'd get us and didn't see the need to rush. It was unnerving, but it was just a tactic, and I refused to let it get to me.

I glanced at the display above the elevators. They were both several floors away. I mashed the button anyway as I pulled Zey past, heading for the stairs.

The door was still several paces away when I registered movement coming around the corner. Shoving Zey behind me, I gripped the pronged weapon and took a fighting stance. If it had hurt her so badly that she could hardly keep up with me, surely it would do the same to them.

A young man came around the corner, posture relaxed, a messenger bag slung across his chest. He looked up from his cell phone, did a double take, and froze in place. He was kind of gangly, with long brown hair tied up in a topknot. We must've looked crazy—shoeless, disheveled, breathing hard, me brandishing a weird-looking poker thing. The dude clearly didn't know what to do with what he was seeing, but I wasn't completely convinced he wasn't one of those things shifted to look like a human.

The elevator pinged, and the doors slowly slid open. I kept my eyes on him as Zey and I shuffled into the elevator. Mashing the button for the basement level, I didn't relax or lower my weapon until the doors were firmly closed. Then I dropped my arms and took a deep breath.

"Need . . . water," Zey panted, leaning heavily on the wall.

"Of course you do." I rolled my eyes and summoned a gallon container from my storage unit. I had to help her lift it to her lips, but once the liquid started flowing, she was able to take it from me and tip it right back. Some of it spilled down her face and cheeks, but she guzzled most of it. Not a drop was wasted, the spilled parts getting absorbed into her skin.

"You can sense them, right?" I asked, keeping an eye on the doors and the number on the panel as we moved down through the building. "You tried to get us to leave before they showed up."

"Yes, I can sense them when they're within a certain range. But they can sense me too. And they can sense me from further away."

"Why?"

"There are more of them. They combine their senses. It's like . . ." she looked to the side, like she was trying to remember the right word. "The best word you have for it is *teamwork*."

"Great." I sighed.

"It can be, but it is not a good thing for you and me in this situation."

"We're going to have to work on your comprehension of sarcasm. Are we about to be outnumbered when these doors open?" I raised the weapon once more as the elevator slowed one floor above the basement.

"No. They are close but not that close."

The doors slid open to reveal nothing, and Zey snatched the weapon from my grasp as she stepped out. I went to fight her for it on reflex but decided against it. She'd know the best way to use it to inflict the most damage.

"OK, well how far away do we need to get so they can't detect you? How did they find us?" Deal with the most pressing issue first, then figure out next steps.

"It's hard to say." She was walking through the parking garage, looking at the cars and the concrete walls with interest.

"Approximately?" I gritted out as I summoned myself a pair of shoes and a hoodie. It was cold, and it was also a good idea to hide my bright-pink hair.

"Approximately one kilometer. More if more of them come through the portal." She finally turned to face me. "We should take one of these vehicles. It will be faster."

"It would be, but none of these belong to me." I overtook her and headed for the security shutter at the top of the ramp leading to the street.

"We can steal one, then," she huffed. Like I was the one being unreasonable.

"No, we can't," I insisted.

"Yes, we can. I already have the information needed to start the engine."

"Listen," I barked, spinning to face her. "I guarantee you every one of those cars is either spelled or has some other kind of tracking or alarm system on it. Figuring out what anti-theft magic is in use and getting around it will take time we don't have. If we take one, we'll have some pissed-off witch or vamp after us as well as your friends.

This is not the best solution. You're in my fucking world. If you want my help, you need to trust me to take the lead in navigating it. Now tell me anything that will be helpful to lose these assholes or incapacitate them and keep your unhelpful commentary to yourself."

She stared at me, mashing her teeth, clearly not liking what I was saying.

"Or you can take your chances on your own." I shrugged. We were even as far as I was concerned.

"Fine," she huffed, "if we can cross a body of water, it will be more difficult for them to track us. Electricity is the most effective weapon."

As she spoke, her skin did that shimmering thing, and she morphed in a matter of seconds, growing taller, broader. I blinked and suddenly *she* was a *he*. The guy from outside the elevators to be specific. He was taller than me now, and my borrowed sweatpants looked comically short on him, not to mention the T-shirt that was stretched to its limit.

"What are you doing?"

"Longer limbs will make it possible to move faster— cover a longer distance."

With a shake of the head, I summoned another hoodie— my baggiest one—and handed it to her. Him. Whatever!

I keyed in the security code, and the door next to the security shutter beeped. I pushed it open and stepped out into the relatively quiet street. A few people were walking past, and I could hear the sounds of traffic on the main street. No faceless assassins in sight.

"Where can I get my hands on a Taser?" I mused out loud. It was one of the few things that I didn't have in my stash.

"We should go to the place where you found me," Zey said.

"Seriously? I thought we—"

"There are more of these there." He held up the weird pronged weapon.

Without answering, I held up a finger and closed my eyes. The ribbons in my mind shot out and beelined for the alleyway from last night. I knew what I was seeking, had held an identical one moments earlier, and I had its location, so it was easy to summon the weapons. There were seven of them. He tucked most of them into his pockets, and I held on to two.

How many of these had he taken last night? I'd seen the effects of just one moments earlier. No wonder I'd practically had to carry the slight woman into my building.

"What are these called?" I asked.

He frowned slightly, searching for a good translation in his mind. "Zaps," he said dismissively, clearly irritated that I'd even asked as his eyes searched the street behind me. "We should hurry."

Right. Time to evade unwelcome company.

I ran out to the main street, Zey keeping close. It was busier here, cars driving past, people going about their business. I turned left and slowed down so we didn't draw unnecessary attention. If we could cover two blocks and got lucky with the timing, we just might be able to lose them.

Apparently, Melbourne used to be the most livable city in the world. But who the hell knew what that even meant? It was well before I was born, long before the portal in Portland opened and changed the world forever. Now, like most other cities, Melbourne had its safe zones—the one's under House rule—and its not-so-safe zones—No Man's Land. The center of the city was a secure pocket where many worked and lived and functioned much like they would've when it was "the most livable city in the world." But anything south of the river was decrepit, abandoned, and unpoliced.

Maybe one quarter of the extensive tramlines that used to connect the city and surrounding areas was still functional. If we could make it to the end of the second block, we'd hit one of the last remaining tramlines, and it would take us to the very edge of Spirit and Sapphire territory— just on the other side of the bridge. With any luck, we'd bump into someone I knew from the few weeks I'd spent here for work, and they could arrange backup.

Screams erupted behind us, and any hope of slipping away without being noticed went out the window.

"Time to run!" I said as I took off, Zey keeping pace. We were only a block away now. More screams and curses came from behind us, and I took a quick glance to assess the situation.

If I weren't running for my life, I would've laughed until I cried.

Four of Zey's buddies were chasing after us, two of them in their pitch-black, faceless forms and two who had taken human form. I just caught the other two starting to shift, their skin doing that weird rippling thing, before I turned forward again.

I could see what they were trying to do, and it was a good effort, but it just wasn't having the effect I'm sure they were hoping for. Seeing them in their true forms would've been startling and frightening for most people. If I were them, I would've used my skills to blend in too. The problem was that wherever they were from, clothing didn't seem to be a thing.

So, there we were, being chased by a group of totally naked people, boobs, genitals and other dangly bits flapping about everywhere.

A five-pronged projectile flew through the air, so close to my head that it made my hair flick up.

Cursing under my breath, I stopped, turned, and flipped an unoccupied table onto its side. The few people who had been dining alfresco at the cafe were already running away in a panic by the time Zey and I crouched down behind our table.

A *thunk* resounded against the solid wood surface, which vibrated with the impact of one of those murder-forks.

Zey shot up, threw his own prong at our pursuers, and ducked back down. They were definitely aiming for him. I was just collateral in this situation. The next time he darted up to throw a weapon, I used this to our advantage. Leaning to the side, I yanked out the two projectiles that were lodged into the tabletop.

Zey's first throw had missed, but this one connected, hitting a middle-aged man right in his beer belly. I threw both my newly acquired weapons. One missed but the other hit the gangly young blond man, who was trying to help beer belly get to safety, right in his skinny butt cheek. They both fell down in a heap of naked, weirdly rippling flesh.

Two down. Two to go. They were closing in fast, mere feet between them and our flimsy shield. And they had more ammo than us.

A distinct dinging in the distance alerted me to an approaching tram.

In the same moment, several Spirit and Sapphire guards came running towards us. They hesitated, clearly confused by the random group of naked people and the scene they'd walked into.

"Stop them!" I barked at the guards, but they still looked uncertain. "I'm a House official from headquarters in

Sydney. They are intruders in our territory. Detain them now!"

Unfortunately, I'd never met any of the guards I was shouting orders at. Even more unfortunately, Zey threw another zap, and it knocked one of his buddies on his ass. Apparently, being clothed while throwing weapons at naked people made you appear like a bigger threat, because the guards chose to come for us.

"Ah, shit!" I spat as the tram came into view, pulling to a stop at the end of the street. There was no one at the stop. The entire area had cleared out, and that tram would be pulling away in a matter of seconds once people realized the chaos that was unfolding.

The guards started shouting to drop our weapons and get down on the ground. The two remaining naked pains in my ass kept throwing projectiles at us. Some of the guards turned their attention to them, realizing the situation was not what they thought.

Zey darted up and threw his last weapon. It connected, but so did the other guy's—er—woman's. An elderly woman with white hair down to her waist—right around where her tits ended.

I yanked the zap out of Zey's arm and shoved him in the direction of the tram.

"Go! Don't get off until you're across the river!" I shouted. He ran.

I was out of weapons. A zap came sailing past my head, aiming for Zey. It missed us both.

A guard took off after him, but there was nothing I could do about it because another lunged for me in the same moment. I ducked out of his way, and he went for his gun. It would be useless against the others but definitely not against me.

I punched him in the throat, mentally chanting "sorry" but realistically I knew I was probably saving his ass. He was better off being unconscious for a few hours. As he spluttered and wheezed, I kicked him in the stomach—away from me and towards the building. Then I came after him and used the momentum to knock his head against the brick wall. He fell in a heap.

I was turning before he even hit the ground.

Zey was nearly at the end of the street. The tram was coming to a stop. The guard that had gone after him was as incapacitated as the one I'd had to deal with. I prayed to all the known and unknown deities that he wasn't dead.

The one remaining naked pursuer was busy fending off three other guards, but a few others were stirring.

Taking advantage of everyone's distraction, I ran. Zey was nowhere to be seen, so I was pretty sure he'd made it onto the tram. I pumped my legs as hard as I could and jumped over the guard lying in the street. The doors started closing. I pushed harder, my lungs burning.

There was no time to slow down; I collided with the half-closed doors and only just managed to shove my arm through the gap, stopping them from closing. The safety mechanism kicked in, and they opened. The other people on the tram grumbled and swore at me—some of them scared of the situation on the street, others just pissed that I was delaying the tram.

I didn't care. I scrambled aboard and jabbed the button to close the doors as I looked back to check on our pursuers.

"Shit," I swore and jabbed it some more. All the guards were lying around unconscious or dead, and two of Zey's buddies were running right for me. They'd dropped the human forms, sailing towards the open tram doors as their black, faceless selves.

The people on the tram scrambled to the other side, alarmed.

The doors started to close—so painfully slow.

They were closing in—too damn fast.

During the chaos, a thought had started niggling in the back of my mind—a memory from a visit to a museum. A few years ago, during some rare time off, my bestie Lowell and I had visited a museum dedicated to policing before the portals had changed everything and the Houses took over. One of the displays allowed visitors to fire a Taser—something commonly used by police back then.

With little more than the memory of the bulky weapon in my grip, I sent my power out urgently. I released an almost maniacal laugh when a Taser appeared in my hand. I had no idea where it had come from, how old it was, or if it would even work.

Taking a step back so my arms wouldn't block the door, I raised it and fired.

CHAPTER 4

I t hit the closest faceless thing right in the chest, mere
feet away from the tram.

Its whole body spasmed, and it fell to the ground,
spasming some more. The other one stopped in its tracks,
then backed up a step, taking in its buddy and following the
wires of the Taser back to me.

The doors closed just as I threw the trigger end of the
Taser through them. The tram took off.

I sagged against the railing, catching my breath for a
moment. The other passengers stared but avoided me.

I stood up straight, gave them all a polite smile like
nothing was amiss, and took the nearest seat. Where the
hell was Zey? A glance around the tram had me frowning.
I'd seen him jump on moments before I did. Did he get back
out through another door? I looked around again, checking
each person, but the gangly young man with the long brown
hair was nowhere to be seen.

An older woman with short blonde hair streaked with
silver sat down next to me.

"That was close," she said, her blue eyes staring at me like she knew what the hell that clusterfuck was all about.

"Uh, yeah, it was . . ." I took in the sweatpants, the too-big hoodie, the bare feet. I leaned in, our noses nearly touching. "Zey?" I whispered.

The corner of her mouth twitched, amusement sparking in her eyes.

I leaned away, my body tensing once more.

The older woman frowned. "Relax. Yes, it's me."

"How do I know you're not one of them?" I mentally ran through everything I had in my storage facility. Surely there was something I could use against these bastards.

"Oh, that." She waved an elegant hand dismissively. "None of them have my charming personality."

I raised one eyebrow. I was exhausted, but I reached out with my power, hoping I could summon one of the zaps I'd left embedded in the naked weirdos chasing us.

The woman sighed and rolled her eyes. "You found me in an alley last night. You like to sleep in shorts and a T-shirt. You saw me shoot myself in the head this morning."

All true. All things that had happened before the others had dropped in unannounced. Plus she was wearing the same clothing I'd put her in. I relaxed.

The tram made another stop. Most of the people got off. It was the last stop before it crossed the bridge into No Man's Land. I watched the doors intently, but no naked people or guards rushed in.

We rode the rest of the way in silence and got off as soon as we were over the bridge. These days, the trams only went one stop further before turning back anyway.

The south side of the river was nowhere near as busy. The few people that we did come across were—for lack of a better word—rough. The buildings were crumbling.

I led us along the river, figuring it was a good idea to stay close to the water in case we needed to lose Zey's buddies again. I could imagine how lovely this area must've been once—when restaurants and cafes lined the wide-open space next to the river.

We passed a homeless human, his milky eyes bugging out as he ranted at us about something. I just sidestepped him. He was drunk, not dangerous.

Once we were out of his sight, Zey shifted. His skin did that rippling thing, and the elegant lady turned into the ranting human. He didn't even miss a step.

That was going to take some getting used to.

He began, "We need to start searching—"

"We need to get somewhere safe and make a plan, and you need to stop doing that."

"Doing what?" A million wrinkles formed on Zey's latest face as he frowned.

"Changing forms constantly. It's distracting."

"I'm only—"

"Shut up."

"Do not tell me to shut up. You are being very rude."

I stopped and faced him fully. I did *not* need this shit. "Yeah, OK, good point. Good luck out here on your own. Bye!" I waved over my shoulder as I started walking again.

He kept pace easily. There were more people, more suspicious eyes, as we got closer to the entrance of what used to be a hotel and casino.

"I will be quiet, but we must hurry," Zey said, leaning close to my ear.

I gave him a withering look and marched inside.

There was a market set up in an open area with a high ceiling. People milled about buying food, clothes, weapons, and things that were hard to find in more reputable places.

House territories had markets and stores, of course, but the markets in No Man's Land were a free-for-all. In places like this, simple healing potions and VitaBrew were sold right next to torture spells, viloss dust, and prostitutes of all species.

As it was in No Man's Land, there was nothing illegal about it because it was nothing that the Houses cared to police. But since I was heading up the project to expand Spirit and Sapphire's territory in the Melbourne area, it was smart to know these kinds of things were around.

I checked the time and sighed. I was supposed to be in a meeting about how many extra guards we'd need to recruit to patrol the expanded perimeter of the territory. Worst morning ever.

We made our way through the crowd and to the stairs leading to the hotel rooms. Several shifters loitered by the door. It was not a hotel anymore—they didn't service the rooms or take bookings—but you had to get through them to gain access.

"Need a room for a couple of hours," I said to the closest one. "How much?"

He looked me up and down. "For you, I'll give you a good price. Two angel feathers and you can pick any room."

"Everyone picks whatever room is free." I crossed my arms. "And I know for a fact you let people up for half that."

His buddies chuckled and the dude grumbled something resembling an agreement and held his hand out. I summoned the three vials of shifter blood I'd made last night—the equivalent of one angel feather in this area—then I reached into my pocket and dropped them into his palm as we walked past.

We had to climb two flights before we found an unlocked room. After the first set of stairs, Zey transformed into the shifter who'd just tried to fleece me. I glared at him and kept going. I needed to get somewhere safe and just fucking think for a minute.

Once the door was safely locked behind us, a chair wedged under the handle for good measure, I took a few moments to breathe.

Zey headed straight for the bathroom, and I heard the shower turn on. I was surprised this place still had running water.

I stared out the window at the city on the other side of the river, getting my shit together, until the shower turned off.

Zey came out nude and looking like the petite blonde I'd first found in the alley. I dragged a hand down my face.

"You can't keep changing forms constantly. It's freaking me out, and I have enough bullshit to deal with. Because of you!" I was a little worked up. Could you blame me?

"Alright." She nodded, and her skin started to do that rippling thing. Waves of deepest black flowed over her skin, and she changed before my eyes. Her hair shortened. Her shoulders widened and rounded out and she grew . . . and grew and grew until I was looking up at her. Him. She'd shifted into a man again.

I frowned and took in the features—the blue eyes, the muscular physique.

"Is this better?" he asked in a very familiar voice.

"Oh my fucking god," I breathed as I realized whose form he'd chosen to take. A carbon copy of Chris Hemsworth—a popular actor from a very long time ago—stood before me. Naked.

I lowered my gaze. It couldn't be helped. My eyes just went there of their own accord, and *oh my fucking god*, I was staring at Chris Hemsworth's dick.

"No!" I shook myself out of it and forced myself to stare at the table on the other end of the room. "This is not better!"

"Why?" He seemed genuinely concerned. "This is the form you find most appealing, isn't it? Your physiological response indicates as much. I thought this would put you most at ease."

Stupid shapeshifting alien man. I slapped a palm to my forehead and sat heavily on the bed.

"You can't walk around with a famous person's face. You'll draw too much attention. We're supposed to be hiding, remember?" I sighed.

Chris Hemsworth cocked his head to the side. "Famous . . ." he muttered, then nodded, looking sad.

We didn't have time to unpack that.

"Can you change into your original form, please?" I said, patting the bed next to me. He shifted as he took the two steps needed to get to me, and by the time he sat down, I was looking at unfathomable blackness and that optical illusion of a face.

The urge to reach out and touch that pitch-black skin was strong. Was it even skin? Did they have skin? The more answers I got, the more questions popped up in my mind. I wanted to know all I could about Zey and where he was from. I wanted to look, touch . . . but I resisted.

"How does this shifting thing work exactly?" I asked. "And how did you even know to turn into Chris Hemsworth in the first place? The man has been dead for decades, so I know we didn't pass him on the street. And come to think of it, why can you speak English? There's no way you speak the same language in . . . uh, where are you from?"

"My world is called Vuulectus," he answered in my

mind. "*And no, we do not speak English there. I learned it last night.*"

"You learned an entire language in a few hours?" I raised my eyebrows.

"*Yes. We call it . . . intuitive learning is the best translation. I heard it being spoken, and my mind filled in the rest. Intuitive learning is also how I chose the form of Chris Hemsworth. I have been observing you and your conscious and unconscious reactions to various stimuli. I deducted that his particular form would be most appealing to you.*"

"Like deductive reasoning on steroids," I muttered. Sounded like it would be a handy thing to have. "Wish my brain could do that."

"*It cannot. You do not have the necessary biological and supernatural components.*"

"Yeah, thank you, Captain Obvious."

Zey cocked that faceless, glowing head to the side, but I kept speaking before he could ask me who Captain Obvious was.

"You can shift into pretty much anything right? You just use real people as a kind of template? So theoretically, you could pick different features and combine them to make your own version of a human?"

"*Correct. I can alter my shape to perfectly resemble any sentient being, but I cannot mimic their power.*"

"That's what I think you should do. Shift into a unique human—someone that doesn't look entirely like anyone else."

"*Fine.*" Was I detecting sass in the voice being projected into my head? "*Which features would you like me to have?*"

"Do I have to do everything?" I threw my hands up with a huff. He just stared back at me with that eyeless face. "Just . . . I don't know. What features do you want? What would the human version of Zey look like?" I stopped just short of saying "just be yourself."

Zey was silent and unmoving for several moments. I waited as patiently as I could, resisting the urge to bark at him to hurry up. Then that depthless black started to ripple, and a more human form began to shape itself.

He stood up as human features slowly started to take shape—much slower than any other transition I'd seen so far. He was really putting thought and effort into this. And he was a *he*.

Zey remained the same height as his true form and chose a lean, athletic build. His shoulders were defined but not bulky, his chest and stomach following the same rules—distinct, strong, but not bulging. Dark hair appeared on his legs and forearms, then almost as an afterthought, a sprinkling on his chest too, with a snail trail leading from his belly button down to—

Nope! I forced myself to look at his face as the features came into focus. A strong brow, a straight nose, a five-o-clock shadow surrounding full lips. The hair on his head, like on the rest of him, was dark, but not quite black, and was cut short with a bit more length on top. He'd chosen tanned, olive skin and even added a tattoo to his left shoulder.

He left his eyes to last, and I stared as the last defining feature of human Zey locked into place. For his eye color, he chose that depthless black that was every inch of him in his true form. There was nothing natural or human-looking about it, but before I could point this out, he added one last detail. Tendrils of amber spread through the black, veining through it like marble. At a glance, it made his eyes appear dark brown.

Had he intentionally chosen my exact eye color to infuse into his? Why would he do that?

I turned away and summoned more clothing for him. The sweats were filthy, and my fave oversized hoodie was ruined. I handed him a pair of shorts and a stretched-out T-shirt I sometimes slept in. Then I remembered the running shoes a guy I'd been sleeping with left behind at my place. They looked about the same size.

"I need to get in touch with my House and report in, sort this whole mess out," I said as I handed him the pile of clothes. "And you need to start talking. Who the hell are those . . . people? And what did you do to make them so mad?"

"Why do you assume I did something? I could be the victim here." He quirked a brow, pulling the T-shirt on over his head. Corded muscle moved under the smooth skin of his torso as he dressed. For the brief moment when his eyes were covered by fabric, I glanced down. I couldn't help myself! It was just *there*, hanging between toned thighs, half-erect, perfectly straight, wonderfully—

"Did I make a mistake?" Zey asked, making me snap out of the staring contest I'd gotten into with his dick. "I formed every part of this body to the ideal proportions."

Yes, he had.

"What? No, it's fine." I shook myself out of it. "I'm pretty sure there's not a single fiber of that bizarre being of yours that's ever been a victim. So out with it. What did you do?"

"They're the ones that did something." He pulled the shorts on, then the shoes. They fit great. "I'm the only one who can undo it. They'll kill me to keep that from happening. And I'll die before I fail to right what they've made so wrong."

I blinked at him. That was intense.

"OK." I sighed and summoned my cell phone. "You can finish your epic speech—with way more detail—after I make this call." I'd ignored two calls, and I had multiple messages. I really needed to check in.

I unlocked the screen and pressed the button to call Reginald Reyes back. Just as it started to ring, Zey sprang forward, yanked the phone out of my hand, and threw it to the other side of the room.

"Hey!" I shoved him in the chest. "What the fuck?"

He grabbed my wrists and fixed me with an intense stare. "You can't call anyone. I told you. There is no time to waste. The Lineg Legion will find us again eventually. We need to get moving."

I stepped closer, spreading my arms and twisting my wrists to get out of his grip. Then I punched him in the throat. On most human men, and many supernatural ones, it would've broken his windpipe. Zey just coughed lightly. It could've been mistaken for a low laugh—especially coupled with the amusement in his eyes.

"Don't break my things," I gritted out. "And don't grab me like you own me. I am so sick of your shit. If you're in such a rush, then go!"

I pointed to the door. Let him run. He wouldn't get far once the witches of the House of Spirit and Sapphire decided to find him. If his buddies didn't get to him first.

He took a measured step back, his arms held up in front of him. I had a feeling it was all the apology I was going to get.

"I cannot go without you."

"Why?"

"I need you." His jaw clenched—such a human reaction. He looked like it physically pained him to say that.

"Find another barely human woman to torture." I ran my hands through my hair. Or at least I tried. My fingers got caught in the tangles. I hadn't had a chance to brush it or take a shower or even have coffee.

"There isn't time. You said it was rare, what you can do. With the Lineg in pursuit and my unfamiliarity with this . . . place," he looked around with a mildly disgusted look on his face, "I cannot afford to lose time."

"Oh, so you're only sticking with me because of my ability? I guess it's not my winning personality then. Bummer."

He frowned. "You are also a proficient warrior. It has been useful already."

"Oh my!" I gasped and held my hands to my chest, using the most mocking voice I could muster, knowing full well that it would completely go over his head. "That's the nicest thing anyone's ever said to me."

"That is . . . unfortunate."

"Yeah, so's that T-shirt." Never mind that the T-shirt was mine. It looked ridiculous on him, and it was making me feel mildly better to throw insults he could hardly comprehend. It was soothing the rage in my belly.

"What?"

"Nothing. Who are these buddies of yours? These liney-whatever?" I demanded.

"They call themselves the Lineg Legion. They are a small group of dissenters from Vuulectus. They are trying to steal a great power for their own selfish gain—a power that belongs to all Vuulectians." His fists were clenched at his sides, and he'd gone super tense. Whatever they'd done had really pissed him off.

"You want me to find something. What is it?" What could he possibly be looking for on Earth when he'd only just stepped foot onto the planet last night?

"When the portal opened, certain things came through it before I did. Things that are crucial to the survival—"

Shouts and bangs came from the other side of the door, making us both whip our heads towards it.

"Your buddies?" I asked, keeping my voice low as I moved silently to look through the peephole.

"No. I would be able to feel their presence."

Hopefully the commotion was unrelated to us. I couldn't see anything but the door on the opposite side of the hallway, but the shouts and bangs kept coming.

When the ruckus reached us, and I saw the familiar blue armbands that members of Spirit and Sapphire sometimes wore on official business, I breathed a sigh of relief and removed the chair from under the handle.

I didn't have a chance to open the door for them though. They just blew through it, making me stumble back.

"Ease up!" I coughed. "I was just about to—hey!"

The Spirit and Sapphire guards ignored me, grabbing me by the arms. I recognized the witch that stepped through the door last. Marina was based in Melbourne and specialized in protection spells. She was average—in appearance and personality—and she was ambitious. We'd met only a few times prior to this project, but I'd been working with her closely these past few weeks. She was local, and her specialty and expertise were useful in setting up the new territory borders.

"What the hell, Marina? Tell them to release me."

There were four guards trying to contain Zey, and they were struggling.

Marina muttered a spell, and magic bands wrapped around Zey, pinning his arms to his sides. Then she turned a flat look to me.

"I'll do no such thing. You failed to report a new portal,

assisted an unknown creature in evading House representatives, and injured several innocent people along the way."
She turned on her heel and marched back out the door. Zey
and I were dragged along behind her.

I cursed internally the entire ride to the House of Spirit
and Sapphire offices in Melbourne. Could this morning get
any fucking worse?

CHAPTER 5

My shoulder was sore from how roughly I'd been dragged out of the van and into this "meeting room" in the basement. Someone was going to pay for that once all this shit was sorted out. I needed to speak to Reginald. I may not have been a powerful witch or a centuries-old vamp or any kind of supernatural at all, but I'd busted my ass to get to where I was. Reg trusted me and I had influence in the House of Spirit and Sapphire. Not bad for a human with a single ability.

They'd cuffed me to a metal bar that was bolted to the wall next to a table. At least they'd been gracious enough to give me a chair. The cuffs dug into my wrists, and I sighed, resisting the urge to take them off. I had a key in my storage that would open these. I could get out of here whenever I wanted, but I figured that running would just make me look more guilty. I had to be patient and play the good little captive until I could get this mess straightened out.

Patience had never been something that came easily to me. It couldn't have been more than ten minutes since I was dumped in this windowless room and left alone, but it felt like hours. I needed to know what was going on. My position within the House of Spirit and Sapphire usually allowed me that knowledge whenever I wanted it. This was practically torture for me.

Thankfully, it was only a couple more minutes before the door opened and Marina walked in with two others. I didn't recognize either and couldn't tell what kind of supe they were. There were a lot of witches in the House of Spirit and Sapphire, but there were plenty of other types too.

"Reginald has portaled in from Sydney. We'll wait for him to arrive," Marina said, taking a seat across from me and scrolling through something on a tablet.

"Good." I nodded, holding back the sigh of relief. "This can be sorted out more efficiently now."

I lived in Sydney at the Spirit and Sapphire headquarters. I knew only a handful of the House members here, so it was no wonder they took Marina's lead. But Reginald Reyes was a powerful warlock and reported directly to Odin and Lady Gabriella. His authority was unquestionable.

I didn't get so much as a glance from any of them, but then Reginald walked into the room.

As usual, he wore an impeccable suit and tie, his salt-and-pepper hair neatly combed back. A custom-made tie clip with a neat row of sapphires held his tie in place.

"Mr. Reyes." Marina sprang to her feet and thrust her hand out. "We haven't officially met yet. I'm Marina—"

"This is hardly the time for pleasantries," Reginald cut her off, and I stifled a smirk. He hated ass-kissers. "Please fetch me a VitaBrew, Mary."

"It's Marina." To her credit, she stood her ground. "And as I'm the senior-most member of Spirit and Sapphire in attendance, other than yourself, I'll have someone else fetch your drink."

Reginald looked her up and down, then grunted with a nod. It was the most approval she'd get from him. She held her head high until he turned his attention to me, then tapped away at her tablet—ordering his drink, no doubt.

"Hey, Reg." I flashed him a tight smile. "You're not gonna believe the morning I've had."

"So I've heard." He unbuttoned his suit jacket and sat across from me. He gestured to my cuffs, and Marina unlocked them from the wall, leaving them around my wrists. Then she took the seat next to Reg, and we all sat in silence while he pulled out his phone and scrolled through some notes. I waited patiently. There was no rushing Reginald Reyes. Especially when it came to procedure.

After a few minutes, he set the device down and sighed. "How long have you been aware of the new portal that opened in the abandoned church around the corner from your apartment building?"

"A couple of hours maybe." I shrugged.

"And how did you come to be aware of it? It opened inside a building and is still concealed."

"Is it? I didn't even know that. I only know there's a portal because I happened across one of the supes from that world and—"

"And when was that?" he cut me off. Reginald was blunt but rarely hostile. A prickle of uncertainty skittered down my spine. Something was not right here.

"Technically, last night just after ten, but I didn't know he—she—was from another realm."

"And you didn't report this?"

"As I said, I thought I was just helping a girl in trouble. Didn't think there was anything to report."

"You left this very building after a meeting just after six, is that correct?" The change of topic took me by surprise.

"Six-oh-eight," Marina supplied helpfully.

"Didn't realize you were keeping track of my schedule so closely." I gave her a withering look. "Yeah, around then."

"And it took you four hours to walk the few blocks back to the apartment?" Reg raised a single brow.

"No. It took me four hours to do whatever the hell I wanted with my free time. What's with the interrogation, Reg?"

"That's what we do when evidence seems to suggest a member of this House has betrayed us." Marina shot me a firm look. "We interrogate them."

"Whoa, what the hell is going on here?"

Reg glanced at me before reaching for his phone again. I could've sworn I saw a hint of disappointment, maybe even uncertainty, in that look. He turned the screen to face me and showed me several images as he spoke. Pictures of me in that damn bar last night.

"Can you explain why you met with a member of the House of Gold and Garnet in No Man's Land last night? What did he hand you? What did you discuss?"

Ah, shit!

"I had no idea he was from Gold and Garnet," I explained, trying my best not to launch myself across the table and strangle Marina. She was clearly having me followed, and she looked way too smug about it.

I explained about the necklace the man was looking for, about my little side-hustle. They both looked skeptical.

Someone came in with two VitaBrews, but my hostile interrogation got back on track as soon as the door had closed again.

Disappointment, frustration, and anger roiled inside me

51

as they sipped their drinks and continued to accuse me of shit I didn't do.

When did I realize I was in the company of a new supernatural species?

Why didn't I report it?

Why had I been ignoring all their calls and messages?

Why did I help him escape to No Man's Land?

Why did I fight members of my own House out in the street?

What were we planning?

How long had we been colluding?

Blah, blah, fucking blah.

With every outrageous question and dismissal of my perfectly honest and reasonable answer, I got more and more pissed.

Twelve years I'd busted my ass to prove myself, to get to a position of respect in the House of Spirit and Sapphire. Twelve. Years. And my word was still not worth shit. They were treating me like a criminal and not listening to me at all.

I tried not to be hurt by the cold, dismissive look in Reg's eyes. He was just my boss; I hardly even liked him as a person anyway. But he'd been my direct superior for five years now. We worked closely on a lot of things. I thought we had—if not a friendship—then at least some semblance of mutual respect and camaraderie. Yet, here he was, not willing to even lift a finger to help me out of an unfortunate situation that was in no way my fault.

Fucker.

After exactly one hour of this bullshit, Reg checked the time and declared he had a meeting to get to. I was just another item on his to-do list.

"We'll have you transferred to Sydney soon," he said to

me on his way out the door. "Until we figure out this situation with the new portal and get to the bottom of your involvement, you'll remain under guard."

With that, he left, Marina on his heels.

I kept my face still and breathed through the feelings of betrayal tearing my insides apart. There was no use in getting emotional. Emotions made you sloppy, and I couldn't afford to be anything other than sharp. Because there was no way I was going to just take this lying down.

I rested my head on the brick wall behind me as I shoved my emotions down and locked them up tight. Then I formulated a plan and reached out for the items in my storage facility that I'd need. The ribbons in my mind unfurled and slunk around them immediately, but I left them loose, at the ready.

The next part would be the hardest. I had to wait.

Reg had ordered that I be kept under close watch at all times. He knew me and what I was capable of. But the guard standing by the door didn't and neither did most of the people in the Melbourne office. It was only a matter of time before Reginald had to head back to Sydney—before the guard got bored and tired.

Unfortunately, the guards were switched out every hour; fortunately, it was the same three guards rotating through.

Hours passed. No one came to give me food or water. My resolve hardened. Sometime in the evening—when the office staff would've gone home for the day and everyone else would be tired—I made my move.

The guard startled a little when I shifted to face him. I'd moved so little throughout the day, they'd probably started to wonder why they were even guarding me.

"Hey, I need to go to the bathroom," I said as I

summoned a little key. The exact key that would fit into the lock on these cuffs.

"You're not to leave this room," he said, voice flat.

"Seriously?" I laughed, using the sound to cover the click of the lock and the cuffs opening. "I've been in here all damn day. I will quite literally piss myself all over this chair if I can't go to the toilet in the next five minutes."

The guard sighed and glared at me. I held his stare and slowly raised one eyebrow in challenge.

"Fine," he grumbled. "I'll need to get another guard."

"Ooh! Two big strong men to escort little old me? I'm flattered."

"It's just orders." He turned, opening the door magically coded to only unlock at his unique signature. I didn't have anything in my stash that would bypass that. I needed him to open that door.

But I did have a powerful sedative. The powder was sold by a fae in Mumbai by the gram. I'd only been able to afford three doses. I summoned one of them into my fist as I dropped the cuffs.

They clattered to the floor as the guard whipped his head around, eyes wide, hand still on the door.

I would've thrown the powder across the room at him, but the fae had been very specific about how the magic worked. I had to blow it into his face or risk being knocked out right along with him.

He reached for the gun at his hip as I sprang forward. He pulled the gun. I lifted my fist, opened it, and blew the dust right into his dumb face.

As he dropped like a sack of potatoes, I lunged for the door that was swinging closed and caught it just in time. I winced as it hit my fingers, jamming them momentarily against the frame. Nothing was broken, and the adrenaline was dulling the pain. Time to move.

I had twenty minutes at best before the next guard came to take over, and I had to be long gone before then. No time to waste, I used the guard's hand to keep the door open a crack, then I summoned a change of clothes. Changing my appearance would hopefully buy me a few extra moments if I happened to run into anyone. Plus sweats and a T-shirt wasn't exactly the most practical outfit for escaping and being a bad bitch in general.

A precious few minutes later, I was in black pants and boots with a long-sleeved shirt and my hair braided up under a cap. The bright pink hair wasn't ideal for not drawing any attention, but there wasn't much I could do about it.

I pushed the prone guard out of the way of the door with my foot and took his gun, tucking it into the waistband of my pants.

A cautious glance through the door showed an empty corridor, and I slid out of the room. There were probably cameras somewhere, even though there hadn't been one in the room, but there was no way to know if anyone was watching them. I forced a steady, measured step as I walked up the corridor like I had somewhere to be.

There was no one around at all, and I wondered if it was really going to be this easy. I followed the illuminated exit signs on the ceiling, spaced between the fluorescent lights, passing an occasional unmarked door.

I made it to the fire escape door without incident. It was across from a set of double doors with windows in the top half. Approaching it with caution, I glanced through the window. It was some kind of machine room, containing what I assumed was the machinery needed to run the heating, cooling, and ventilation to the entire building.

A figure was facing the door, chained between two massive machines, its depthless black form slumped, its arms tied wide apart. I knew it was Zey, even in this form. His T-shirt was ripped at the neck.

Like he'd sensed my gaze, he lifted his head a fraction, those unnerving lights where a face should be angled in my direction.

He did that rippling thing, but he was clearly not in a good way and not able to shift forms. All he managed was a momentary partial shift. His face—the face he'd chosen for himself that morning—flickered into place, and those eyes connected with mine. His expression was stoic, if strained, but his eyes burned with intensity.

It was barely a split second and then it was gone, his true form back in place. The four guards facing him at attention didn't even seem to notice.

What did that look mean? Was he hoping I was coming to rescue him? Or was he about to alert them to my escape so he could use their distraction to get away himself?

I didn't wait to find out.

Turning on my heel, I pushed the fire door open and started climbing. There were no stairs down, confirming my suspicion that we were underground. Two flights of stairs brought me to an external door.

I couldn't be sure it wasn't spelled to raise an alarm if it was opened, but I didn't have time to worry about it. For all I knew, Zey's guards were already heading for me as he made his own escape.

I rushed out into the chilly Melbourne night. The door slammed closed behind me as I picked up my pace, needing to get as far away from the building as possible.

It started to drizzle lightly, and a teeny-tiny pang of guilt shot through my chest as the rain made me think of Zey. He'd surely turn his head up to the sky, soaking every fine droplet in through that weird skin of his.

At the edge of the lane, I glanced back. The area was empty, the building quiet. I peeked around the corner to the front doors. Light spilled out onto the street from the lobby where a guard stood smoking a cigarette and scrolling through his phone. Surely all guards would've been called back if they'd realized I was missing.

Zey hadn't ratted me out after all.

With no time to question my decisions, I turned and started walking in the opposite direction. He'd shown up and turned my life upside down out of nowhere. I didn't owe him anything. I had to take care of myself—no one else would. That's how it had always been, and this situation couldn't be any different.

I was doing what I had to do.

If our places were reversed, and it had been you chained up in that basement, would you have ratted him out to get yourself free? A small, irritating voice in the back of my head asked.

I would've done what I had to do. I was not going to go down for something I wasn't guilty of.

But he'd stayed silent. He'd allowed you to escape.

I gritted my teeth, beyond pissed that I was feeling even a *little* bit guilty for leaving him down there. What the hell was I supposed to do? I was good, but I wasn't take-on-four-guards-at-once-on-my-own good. We both would've ended up in chains.

I forced the thoughts out of my mind and concentrated on my surroundings.

The streets were busy with people on their way to dinner or leaving work late, but they weren't packed.

The group of people crossing the street on a diagonal were not easy to miss. I slowed my steps as I realized what was happening.

They were heading straight for the front doors of the building I'd just busted out of. And they were clearly Vuulectians.

It was a ragtag group of about a dozen people of varying ages and builds. They'd figured out that adult bodies were stronger and faster than little kid bodies, so they had all taken the forms of healthy, capable adults. But while they'd also figured out that nudity tended to draw people's attention, their clothing of choice was a dead giveaway. They were all shoeless and only a few had socks on. The clothing they'd stolen was ill-fitting and mismatched, dresses and sweatpants clashed with too-tight T-shirts and sparkly jackets.

I would've known it was them even without spotting a few of them doing that rippling thing with their skin as they absorbed the rain that was falling heavier with every moment.

They were going after Zey. And judging by previous interactions with this lovely group of individuals, absolute chaos was about to erupt in that building. I couldn't have asked for a better distraction to cover up my escape and ensure it went unnoticed until I was long gone.

Or...

Cursing under my breath the whole way, I rushed back to that fire door. Then I pulled out my gun and waited. Sure enough, only a few moments later, guns started going off, shouts rang out, even an alarm started wailing. Chaos.

I shot the lock of the door, which only opened from the

inside, and yanked it open. Questioning my life choices, I hurried down the two flights of stairs and peeked through the door. The hallway was empty, so I moved to the double doors on the other side and looked through the window.

Zey was in the same spot and the same condition but only one guard remained. The others would've been called away, as I suspected. I could handle one.

I summoned one of the big jugs of water from my stash and marched into the room.

"Hey, dude!" I called, totally casual, like there wasn't a siren blaring and an active attack on the building a few floors above. "I'm totally lost."

The guard turned to face me, tense but confused. His momentary bewilderment bought me the few moments I needed to cross the large room.

He reached for his weapon, but I was faster. I swung the jug and whacked him on the side of the head. He stumbled. I summoned my favorite knife, stabbed a hole in the jug, and threw it in Zey's direction.

The guard righted himself and pulled his gun, his eyes flashing a bright yellow for a moment. Shifter. Dammit! I wasn't sure which kind, but they were all tough bastards. He wouldn't be as easy to take down as I'd hoped.

I kicked the gun out of his hand before he could aim it and swiped at him with my dagger. He dodged out of the way and threw a meaty punch. I darted back but not fast enough to avoid the hit altogether. He caught me in the ribs, knocking the breath out of me.

He grabbed my arm and swung for my head this time. He was bigger and stronger, but I was faster, and I had nothing left to lose. I ducked and twisted under his arm, breaking his grip, before punching him in the side of the head. It was a blow that would've knocked most people out, but this shifter just grunted and turned his snarling gaze on me.

I feinted to the left, then darted right and gripped his shoulder. Using him as leverage, I climbed the side of a machine with swift steps until I was hanging off his back like a monkey. One arm went around the front of his neck while the other anchored it and pressed against the back of his neck in a chokehold.

He tried to shake me off, but I squeezed my thighs around his waist and my arms around his neck and stayed glued to him. He started struggling for air and flailing about, making sloppy attempts to hit me and get me off him. I had a foam pad ready to summon when he started stepping backwards, probably looking for a wall to slam me against, but his movements were more stumbling than anything.

I took a glance in Zey's direction. The water was spilling out of the jug and onto the ground right next to where he knelt, and he was absorbing every drop through his legs. His face was turned in our direction, and the lights in it looked brighter already. Good. We didn't have time to spare for him to guzzle water and recover before he could move. His skin rippled as his chosen form came into focus.

I concentrated on planting my feet to the ground as the shifter guard started to go down. His arms went limp, and his body followed suit. I held on for another few moments to make sure he was out, then lowered him to the ground.

By the time I rushed over to Zey, he was fully shifted into his male self, his black-as-night eyes boring into me. I inspected his shackles, summoned a key that would work, and freed him. He grabbed the jug, opening his mouth wide, and poured the rest of the water down his throat in one go. He didn't even pretend to swallow.

"The Lineg are one floor above us." He glanced up at

the ceiling. "On the other side of the building, but we don't have much time."

"Better get gone then." I ran to the door. A glance out the windows confirmed we were alone down here, and I grabbed the handle. It didn't budge.

"Fuck!" I yelled, pulling my hand back like the handle had burned it, even though all I'd felt was a light zap.

"What is it?" Zey's wide eyes swung between the door and my hands.

"The door is spelled. It won't open for us," I spat, feeling beyond frustrated that I didn't think to prop it open with something on my way in, and beyond pissed off that I'd ruined my own escape. "And because I'm not someone who the spell recognizes, it would've sent an alert to whomever set it up." Which could be Odin himself, considering the seriousness of the situation.

"Perhaps there is another way out." Zey turned toward the other end of the room—the one that was nothing but concrete. I grabbed his sleeve and kept him by my side.

"There is." I sighed. I'd hoped not to have to use this way out. I only had one, and it had been nearly impossible to get. I was saving it for the most dire of situations. Unfortunately, I thought this qualified.

We had no way out of this room without a witch to break the spell on the door. Zey's buddies were closing in. Whoever had been notified when I tried to open the door was surely mere moments away too.

I held my hand out and summoned a gabbro stone containing a one-way portal.

A portal appeared before us, swirling with magic at the edges, just big enough for a person to step through. Verdant green and dappled sunlight was visible beyond.

The double doors slammed open, and several people

rushed inside just as I took Zey's hand and we stepped through.

I glanced back as the portal closed in on itself. Marina stood among shocked, angry people on the other side. She looked beyond surprised—she looked disheveled and overwhelmed and *seething*. I almost felt sorry for her.

The portal closed with one last spark of magic, before that too fizzled to nothing.

CHAPTER 6

T bent over, resting my hands on my knees, and heaved in breaths. That was close—too close. At least I knew I'd made the right call by using the one portal I had. If we'd been caught again, we wouldn't have been able to escape. Our security would have tripled, and we'd probably be moved to a facility with much stronger containment spells.

"Where are we?" Zey asked, looking around at the forest. Springtime had the area feeling particularly alive and vivacious. We stood on a narrow hiking track, nothing to see or hear but nature—trees swaying, birds chirping, running water somewhere in the distance.

"Very far away from the multiple assholes chasing us." I stood up straight and propped my hands on my hips, still catching my breath. Zey was breathing hard too, and all he'd had to do was chug water and step through a portal. What the hell had they done to him? I scanned him for injuries. Not that I knew what an injury on someone from his realm even looked like.

"I cannot sense the Lineg at all. We must be far indeed." He was staring into the woods, his eyes searching.

"Good. Finally."

"They will find us. It may take longer now, but they will." He fixed me with that intense look of his.

"Yeah, well—"

He walked off the path into the woods where he'd been staring.

"Hey!" I called after him as I followed. "That's not where we need to go."

"I need water."

I rolled my eyes. "I can summon you more water."

"No need. There is plenty here." He ducked under a branch, and when I followed, I found that the running water was much closer than I thought. A small river cut through the dense forest, hardly more than a brook.

Zey dropped his pants, flashing me his annoyingly toned ass. His T-shirt followed, and he waded into the water. It reached his thighs when he was at the deepest section. He dove under and remained below the surface for a long time. If he'd been human, I would've been panicking that he'd drowned. Shit! Maybe he *was* drowning. Just because he needed water to repair and whatever didn't mean he couldn't get too much of it. Humans needed water to live too, and we could still drown.

"Zey!" I shouted, moving to the very edge of the river and scanning the surface. The running stream splashed against the toes of my boots. "I did not go through all that, saving your ass, only for you to fucking drown in a thigh-deep brook!"

His head popped up a few feet downstream and he flashed me a grin. It was the first smile I'd seen from him, and it was . . . startling.

"I'm quite well, Sky," he said, standing to his full height. Water dribbled down his body, and his hair was stuck to his scalp. He must've finally sated his insatiable thirst if his skin was no longer absorbing water.

He started wading towards me, his powerful thighs cutting through the rushing water, his manhood bouncing between them.

I huffed and turned away. *Manhood?* Ugh! I crouched and scooped water into my hands, having a good drink myself. The water was refreshing, if a little too cold, and felt like silk sliding down my throat.

A pair of bare legs moved into my range of vision, water now flowing around the ankles.

I glanced up, forcing myself to ignore the *manhood* mere inches from my nose. Zey was watching me with a curious expression.

"You can only ingest water through your mouth? How do you get enough?"

"We don't need as much as you apparently do. Can you please put some damn clothes on?" I drank more water.

"Why are you all so bothered by nudity? It's only your natural form," he asked. Thankfully I heard the rustle of clothing as he spoke.

"Centuries of patriarchy," I said as I stood up.

He gave me that curious tilt of his head, his brow furrowed. After a few moments, his brows rose high, and then a look of bewildered disgust settled on his face. "That is a horrible system of society, not to mention inefficient."

"Couldn't agree more," I mumbled, ducking under that tree branch and making my way back to the path. Zey caught up as I started walking up it.

"Where are we going?" he asked.

"Somewhere safe. Hopefully."

"Why?"

"Because," I huffed.

"Sky, we do not have time. We have to start searching for the—"

"No!" I cut him off with a finger in his face and a stern look without breaking my stride. "You skipped off into the woods to have a splash around in the stream because your body needed it. Well, my body needs food and rest and a moment to fucking *think*. So we're going this way where I can get those things. You're making me regret going back for you."

There was a stretch of silence, nothing but the sound of my boots and his bare feet on the dirt path.

"Why did you come back for me?" he asked. "You were out; your absence had not been noted."

"I don't fucking know." I rubbed my forehead. A headache was settling in. "Why didn't you tell them I was escaping? It could've given you a chance to get free."

"I could sense the Lineg coming closer. I hoped that I could get away in the commotion they would create. But that would be pointless with you still imprisoned. I need you to find what I'm looking for."

He let me escape because he needed me for his plan— not because it was the right thing to do. Asshole.

"How much further is this place?" Zey asked. There was a hint of irritation in his voice, but he was smart enough to keep the question sounding casual.

"Maybe another half-hour walk." If I remembered correctly.

"Were you not able to open the portal closer to your destination?"

"Yeah, I could've. But then the people after us would've

immediately recognized the building, and we'd be back to scrambling to escape them."

Zey grunted and I could've sworn it sounded like he was conceding that was a smart move.

"Can you summon a vehicle to get us there faster?"

"Oh, wow!" I slapped my forehead and gave him a wide-eyed look. "That's a *fantastic* idea! Why didn't I think of that?"

His eyes narrowed. "Sarcasm?"

"What do you think?"

"I think it is sarcasm."

I was really regretting saving his ass.

"I would like to know more about your ability," he said, his voice soft and not demanding for once.

"Yeah, I bet you would," I mumbled. I hated being used. "I can't summon things that large. It's limited to things I can hold or pick up. I could summon a scooter, but it will be useless on this terrain. Plus, I don't have a scooter in my storage facility." I made a mental note to add one. It was a mode of transport faster than walking. Could come in handy.

"Could you not just summon one from somewhere else?"

"That would be stealing. I don't steal." The gods knew there had been more people than I cared to remember who had tried to use me for just that. I'm sure it was one of the main reasons I'd been able to join the House of Spirit and Sapphire. No one had said it outright, but there had been hints dropped that if useful or valuable items were to suddenly appear, it would be appreciated. It didn't take long for them to learn I had morals I was not willing to compromise. Thankfully, my ability was still useful in other ways. That and they wanted to keep me close—and therefore out of the clutches of someone else who could use me to steal from them. "And I have to have touched the object, or one identical to it, to summon it."

He stopped in his tracks. "So, you cannot summon things you haven't been in contact with before? You cannot help me after all." He looked furious, like he was prepared to turn around and walk in the opposite direction, leaving me behind without a second thought. But we were in the middle of nowhere, and that path just led further into the woods and eventually looped back around to where we were going. So good luck to him.

I kept walking, grinding my teeth. "No, I can't summon whatever the fuck it is you're looking for."

He caught up and matched my pace once more. "No, but you can find it. That's what you said before right? Just like the witches that can do what you do? You can locate items for people."

"Yep."

"Could you look for what I'm seeking now? While we walk? So I can be on my way."

I guessed he decided I wasn't so useless after all. Anger and frustration bubbled up my throat until I felt like I was choking on it.

"So, you're gonna just drop into my life, completely destroy it, use me to get what you need, and then just disappear, leaving me to clean up the mess you made?" I'd unconsciously picked up my pace, power walking as I ranted. "No! Fuck you, Zey!"

"How have I destroyed your life?" he asked, infuriatingly calm.

"My own people arrested me right along with you! They think I'm helping you in some secret scheme to destabilize the system they have to rule this shitstain of a world.

Because I didn't report in as soon as I realized what you were. Because half of gods-damned Melbourne saw me fighting my own House members and running away with you! Twelve fucking years with the House of Spirit and Sapphire and my word means nothing. Because of you! I'm going to be excommunicated if not imprisoned. My life is ruined!" I screamed that last part so loudly that some birds shot out of a nearby tree.

"I didn't know," Zey said, irritated. That made two of us.

"Of course not. All you care about is finding your precious trinkets and . . . I don't know . . . whatever."

"I would like to propose a deal," he said.

"What?" I shot him a look, confused by the sudden change in topic.

"A bargain. I did not intend to create so much difficulty, Sky. I'm simply trying to do the right thing for my people. But I cannot do that without regard for you . . . for you and *your* people."

"Get to the point, Zey." My patience was paper thin. Like, crepe-paper-dunked-in-water flimsy.

"Help me find what I'm looking for before the Lineg get to it or to me, and I'll help you get your life back."

"How?" I gave him a skeptical look.

"I will go to your people willingly and answer all their questions. I'll tell them everything—that you were not involved, that I dragged you into my mess."

"What makes you think they'll believe you?"

"Once I have the items I need, they won't have a choice."

"Ominous, but OK, then. Why should I trust you? How do I know you won't just use me and disappear as soon as you have what you want?"

"You have my word," he said like it was the end of the matter.

"Your word?" I scoffed.

"My people do not lie or deceive," he said, his voice intense. "At least not the worthy ones."

I had no idea what the hell that meant, but I also had no other options. If he held up his end of the bargain, this nightmare would be over. If he didn't . . . well, I'd be pissed, but I'd be in the same position I was in now.

I had nothing left to lose.

"Fine." I stopped to face him fully and held my hand out. "You have yourself a deal."

He flashed me that grin again, but it was quickly replaced with a frown as he glanced down at my outstretched hand.

"Here, when two people strike a deal," I reached out with my free hand and grabbed his wrist, bringing it up, "they shake hands to seal it. Sometimes there is a magical binding spell involved too, but I don't have a witch handy to cast it, so this will have to do."

His warm hand wrapped around mine and held it firmly but gently. I pumped our joined hands up and down a few times and stilled them. For a few weird moments we just stood there, staring at our clasped hands. I felt so much calmer than I had just moments ago. It must've been because I'd made a decision, had a plan. Still, it was such a sudden change.

I tugged my hand back, and Zey's hold on it tightened for a split second before he released it.

"Now let's go and find out if I have any friends left in this world," I said as I resumed our trek towards Braemar Castle.

CHAPTER 7

Braemar Castle was nestled in the Scottish countryside, tucked in among rolling green hills like it had stood there just as long as the terrain around it. Multiple towers jutted into the sky, and small windows were set into the heavy stone of the structure. A high stone wall surrounded the entire compound.

I'd been here just a few months ago—when my life had been my own and not smashed to pieces by an annoying supernatural from some alien realm. I'd come here as an envoy on behalf of my House. Initially, we were supposed to try to entice the newly discovered phantoms to join Spirit and Sapphire, but that didn't exactly go to plan. Between multiple shocking revelations and betrayals, and something that had caused me great personal pain, it had been an eventful visit.

The people of Braemar Castle had ended up establishing their own House. The House of Death and Diamond had come into existence under unusual circumstances, but I had nothing but respect for the leader who had made it happen. I'd left on good terms with Sabrina and

Kieran, if still a bit formal. I had no idea if I could ask them to hide us or if they'd alert the other Houses immediately.

We were about to find out.

The heavy door set into the stone wall opened. We were still only halfway up the path when Sabrina herself stepped out.

"Sky! What a pleasant surprise!" Sabrina gave me a genuine smile. Her red hair was tied back, and she was wearing activewear and sneakers—like she was about to go for a run.

We met at the top of the path, and the phantom surprised me by tugging me into a hug. She was frowning when she pulled back, having taken in my disheveled appearance and the shoeless, dirty man who was with me.

"Yeah . . ." I cringed. "You may not think it's so pleasant when I tell you why I'm here."

"Come inside." She waved us in without hesitation. "I'll have some tea made."

I shook my head. "It's better if no one knows we're here."

Zey sat in the plush armchair that was furthest from the fire. He was completely still yet somehow managed to look impatient.

Sabrina had led us up a different path to a cabin on her property. It was far enough from the castle that no one would notice us here, and it seemed to be under construction. There were tools and piles of leftover timber and paint cans in one corner of the small porch. It looked like the renovations were pretty much finished because there was furniture in the cabin that smelled faintly of paint, and artwork sat propped up on the floor, waiting to be put up.

We'd made small talk on the walk over and while Sabrina built a fire, so I got straight to the point once we were all seated. "Sabrina, I'm sorry in advance for putting you in this situation, but I'm hiding from the House of Spirit and Sapphire until I can prove something. I need a place to lay low for a night, two max."

"You're hiding from your House?" The genuine shock on her face was all the proof I needed that she genuinely didn't know what was happening. That meant that the House of Spirit and Sapphire was keeping this whole situation quiet. It wouldn't last long. They'd have to tell the other Houses a new portal had opened, and soon. And if they couldn't find me pronto, they'd have to resort to naming me a high-priority fugitive. My face would be plastered all over the Houses' official communication channels. The fact that I'd spent the past twelve years traveling all over the world on various assignments as a representative of the House of Spirit and Sapphire would not work in my favor.

"It's not what I wanted, trust me," I said, forcing myself not to glance in Zey's direction.

"What is it you need to prove? Maybe we can help."

"I promise you, no one can help with this. And the less you know of the details the better."

Sabrina sighed, and I couldn't tell whether she was irritated that I wouldn't let her help or mad that I'd brought a diplomatic mess to her door when her newly formed House was so vulnerable.

"I'm assuming this has something to do with your friend here? Who is he?" she asked.

"He's not my friend, and he's not important," I rushed out.

"I would argue that I'm the most important one in this situation, all things considered."

"You would." I rolled my eyes.

"Sky, I want to help you, but you have to give me something here," Sabrina half pleaded, half admonished, her Scottish accent thickening with her frustration. "I'm sure you can appreciate the difficult position you're putting me in."

"Absolutely I can. And you can definitely say no. All I ask is that you give us a couple of hours head start before you report anything." I went to stand up.

"Oh, sit down." Sabrina rolled her eyes. "You're so dramatic sometimes."

"I am not!" I almost laughed. I didn't think anyone had referred to me as dramatic before.

"I would have to agree with Sabrina, you can be dramatic," Zey added.

"No one asked you, Zey," I huffed. I was, despite my protests, acting a little dramatic with him. Even I had to admit that. But he'd frayed my last nerve, and I'd been surviving on protein bars and my stubborn refusal to give up all day. I was beyond hangry.

He ignored me and addressed Sabrina, leaning forward on his knees. "My name is Zey. I am the reason Sky finds herself in such a difficult situation. It was not my intention, but what's done is done, and all I can do now is prove her innocence. And I would not feel comfortable taking advantage of your hospitality without being honest about the level of risk you'd be undertaking. As well as Sky's House, my people are also in pursuit of us. But I assure you, I will know if they get close, and we will lead them away from your home. I implore you, humbly, please help us."

Sabrina and I both blinked at him. Where the hell was this polite charm when he'd busted into *my* life uninvited?

"Your people are not associated with a House?" Sabrina asked.

I was trying to protect Sabrina by not telling her too much, but Zey was right about one thing—not that I'd admit it out loud. It wasn't right to ask her to help without giving her some info.

"There's a new portal," I said, keeping my voice low. The walls in this place tended to have ears sometimes, as I'd learned on my last visit.

"Shit." She deflated and flopped back against her chair, eyeing Zey with more curiosity and caution.

"One night. And we can pretend we were never here. Please." I swallowed around the lump of tension in my throat. *Please* and *sorry* were not words I found easy to say, *ever*, and I'd said both in one conversation. Zey had better hold up his end of the deal.

"You're lucky Kieran is visiting his uncle and isn't here." She rubbed her forehead then agreed to let us stay.

Sabrina hiked back to the castle and came back with a basket of food, although Zey didn't have any and sipped on water constantly, so I ate most of it. She left us alone then— just me and Zey and one bed that took up half the space, and strict instructions to not leave the cabin.

I locked myself in the bathroom and spent a long time in the shower, letting the hot water work out some of the tension in my body as I turned everything over and over in my head. It was still hard to believe that I was in this situation at all.

For once, Zey left me alone and didn't pester me to find his precious things while I ate and showered and summoned some sweats to change into. It was only eleven in the morning, but with the time difference and the fact I'd been through hell, I was exhausted. But as much as I needed rest, my mind was still racing.

So I figured it was a good time to get more info about what we were searching for.

I opened the door to the bathroom, and Zey was right there on the other side, like he'd been waiting for me.

"You alright there?" I shuffled past him.

"You were in there a long time," he griped.

"Yeah, and now I'm out here. What's your point?" I crossed my arms.

He just stared at me as I moved to the bed. I climbed onto it and leaned back against the headboard.

"I need to know about these things you're trying to find. What are they? What do they look like? What do they do?"

"I do not know what they look like," he stated . . . and didn't elaborate.

I pinched the bridge of my nose. "What? Then how do you know what you're looking for? How do you even know they're here on Earth? Didn't the portal between our worlds only open the other day?"

"It did, yes." He nodded. "These items don't have a physical embodiment usually, and they're not so much items as they are . . . something else. I know they are here because I can feel it."

Frustration was rising again, and I was way too tired to keep it from exploding into a toddler tantrum for much longer. "Zey, I need more than that. I've told you how my ability works and what the limitations are. You need to give me something to work with here. And for the love of the gods, sit down."

He was making me feel unsettled just standing in the

middle of the room. Thankfully he didn't argue, coming to sit at the foot of the bed.

"How much do you need to know to find them?" he asked.

"Without having seen or touched them myself, as much as possible." Even then, I wasn't entirely sure I could do this. The more he revealed about these things, the more I doubted my ability could do anything at all to find them. I wasn't about to tell him that though. Not when my life depended on it. And I sure as hell wasn't about to give up without trying.

"They are called Onuei, and they are at the core of what makes my people what we are. You mentioned patriarchy earlier; well, we used to have similar systems. They were not based on gender but discriminatory and divisive nonetheless. This was a very long time ago. We have peace and harmony now. Our world is not perfect, but it is far better and more advanced than anything you've ever had here on this Earth."

"Rude," I muttered, but honestly human history was a shit show, so I wasn't going to argue.

"Through many generations, we developed a system where all are equal, and our leader is chosen not through a flawed system that can be easily manipulated, but through an ancient magic that seeks out the worthiest individual— the one who best fulfills the people's will and the good of the realm. It's similar to what you might call royalty, but birth does not decide succession. The Onuei determine that."

"How?" I crossed my legs and grabbed a pillow to cuddle in front of me. I was actually kind of riveted by what Zey was telling me. The way his face softened when he spoke about his people, the way his eyes lit up as he explained the system he clearly believed in with his whole being—well it didn't hurt seeing all that either.

"When the True Leader dies, the three Onuei leave his body and go to the worthiest person. That is how we know who the next True Leader is. There is no way to falsify the glow that comes from within an individual for the first week of their ascension to power and responsibility. It is a great, sacred honor, respected by all . . . most." He frowned and his jaw tensed. I leaned forward slightly, totally invested in the story.

"OK, three of them. We can handle that. What do they look like?" I asked before yawning so hard that my jaw ached. Zey started to say something as I settled back against the pillows, but I must've been more tired than I realized. I involuntarily fell into a heavy sleep.

Sometime later, I woke myself up with my own snoring. I jolted into consciousness with a snort and rubbed my eyes. When I opened them, I jolted again, sitting up and summoning my fighting knife.

Zey was sitting in the exact same spot I'd left him when I went off to sleep land.

"You scared the crap out of me!" I chastised as I set the knife down on a bedside table and held my hand to my racing heart.

"I have not moved" was his helpful response.

"Yeah, well . . . whatever." I stretched.

"You leaked while you slept." He looked at the pillow I'd been using, and I followed his gaze to find a patch of drool.

I quickly flipped the pillow over and wiped the corners of my mouth. "That's a totally normal human thing. Happens to everyone. What time is it?"

His lips quirked, amusement showing briefly in those strange eyes.

Before he could answer, there was a knock at the door and we both stood, my knife back in my hand.

Sabrina poked her head in, and I relaxed.

"Only me," she said with an understanding smile before slipping into the room. She was carrying a basket with a checkered tea towel over it.

"I brought dinner." She held the basket up. "I'd invite you to eat with us, but the fewer people know you're here the better."

"Of course." I took the basket from her. "I completely understand. Thank you so much."

"In the morning, I'll give you a ride into a busy town where you or I are less likely to be recognized, but we should leave early, before anyone is up."

"We'll be ready," I assured her.

With a nod and a curious glance at Zey, she left.

I unpacked the contents of the basket onto the desk under the small window—a roast with gravy, vegetables, mashed potatoes, and little Yorkshire puddings. Delicious!

The hills surrounding the castle were bathed in warm afternoon light, the shadows long. I'd slept half the day away and woke up starving and, somehow, tired again.

"Start from the start," I demanded around a mouthful of creamy mashed potatoes.

"A portal opened in Vuulectus many years ago." Zey stayed on the bed, telling me his story as I stuffed my face. "Nothing came through it, and we deemed the risk too great to try ourselves. Until about one year ago, when something did come through it. We are unused to dealing with other species, unintentional mistakes were made, some people died."

"Where does the portal lead to?"

"A story for another time. All you need to know is that our leader made the decision to keep our distance—for the safety of our people. But the ones on the other side of the portal were more curious, more persistent. A small number of Vuulectians disagreed with the True Leader's decision to not engage with this new world."

"Let me guess—Lineg Legion?"

"Precisely. They saw an opportunity to deal and trade with the new world, and did not consider the safety of everyone else, of our way of life. They became greedy for power and resentful of our leader."

He paused and I glanced over to find him frowning at a spot in the distance. He looked sad and angry, and I waited patiently for him to continue.

"I was an advisor to the True Leader. We had been friends from an early age. Several days ago, we were walking through a remote area, an afternoon of leisure after several days of visiting those who were unable to bring their concerns to the True Leader in the capital. We were attacked by the Lineg Legion. They killed the True Leader, nearly killed me also. They had some kind of magical shield —provided by the new world, I'm sure—that prevented the Onuei from being released and finding the one worthy of becoming the new True Leader."

I'd stopped eating. I was full, but also riveted by his story of betrayal and intrigue.

"Unable to go to the worthy one, the Onuei seemed to . . . tear a hole in space and time itself. They somehow opened a new portal, disappeared through it, and hid themselves until they could be found and returned safely to Vuulectus. I followed them through the portal, and you found me not long after I managed to evade the one Lineg who was well enough to follow me."

"Clearly, more of them have come through now." I sighed. Zey nodded. "So, they're after the Onuei too?" I awkwardly shaped my mouth around the unfamiliar word.

"Yes. They are desperate to find them so they can force their power into their leader—an unworthy one who will only use it to manipulate our people. But they know I am here, trying to return the Onuei to their rightful place, and they will hunt me just as desperately to stop that from happening."

Great. I groaned on the inside, wondering if anyone else wanted to join the party. I mean, his people and mine were already after us; what's another couple of dozen?

"How do I know you're not the one who's actually trying to steal the Onuei for your own greedy self?" I blurted.

"I do not lie," he declared, jumping to his feet and glowering over me.

"Uh-huh. How do I know that's not a lie?" I stood up too, refusing to cower. He was taller than me, but I planted my feet and stared him down.

"What do you care?" he scoffed, backing off. "You just want me to clear your name. What difference does it make to you what my true intentions are?"

I watched him skeptically for a moment, then shrugged. "True. OK fine, let's see if I can find your magic balls."

"They are not balls. They don't have a discernible shape. They're pure magic." He still looked like he wanted to challenge me to a duel for insulting his honor, but I was about to do what he wanted, so he moved out of my way as I walked to the bed and climbed onto it.

Keeping everything Zey had told me at the forefront of my mind, I closed my eyes and tapped into my power. The ribbons in my mind floated as if on a gentle breeze, ready to be whipped by a strong wind in the direction of what I sought. But without a visual or anything to go on, they remained where they were, floating in various directions fluidly.

Changing tack, I tried to think outside the box and searched for something that didn't belong, something not of this world. The ribbons shivered and multiplied, some of them unfurling in various directions. I quickly realized that was a bust too. Half the shit on Earth was not of this world since the portals started appearing.

I opened my eyes to find Zey inches from my face, staring at me intently. I gasped and leaned back. How the hell did he move that silently?

"Creep!" My hands went to his chest to push him back.

"Did you find them?" he asked, completely unbothered and unaware of the concept of personal space and totally unmoved by my attempts to shove him away.

"Maybe if you give me some damn space!" I shoved at his chest again.

"Whatever you need." He leaned away immediately, and I dropped my hands. One of them brushed against his bare forearm. Unbidden, the image of a ribbon twining around my hand, binding it gently to Zey's forearm, flashed in my mind.

I wrapped my fingers around his arm, instinctually following my power's lead. "Wait," I whispered, and he froze on the spot. "Don't move."

I let my eyes close, and this time, there was just one ribbon floating on the wind. It was fine as gossamer and felt like it might snap at the slightest pressure, but it was there, and it was unfurling towards . . . something.

Zey had an innate magical connection to the items I was trying to find, and my ability was using that to seek them out. Maybe all people from his realm had a connection to the Onuei, maybe it was just Zey for whatever reason—it didn't really matter.

I opened my eyes, a faint smile pulling at the corners of my lips. Zey had leaned back into my personal space, but I was not startled this time.

"You found them," he said, his own hint of a smile appearing.

"Not exactly. But I know where to look, which direction we need to head in. Your connection to the Onuei helps, and the closer we get, the clearer the location will be."

He grinned. "I knew you could do it."

That made one of us.

"Let's go. Which way is it?" He got to his feet, his absence making me acutely aware of how close our faces had been.

"No." I scrambled off the bed. "I told you I need rest."

He frowned and opened his mouth like he was about to argue, but snapped it shut. I walked to the bathroom, avoiding his gaze.

"I'll let you know when I'm ready," I said as I pulled the door closed behind me.

I was beyond exhausted, especially after pushing my power to do something I hadn't tried before, something I didn't think I was capable of.

After another shower, I tried to rest. The bed was comfortable and warm, but my sleep was fitful regardless. I kept waking up excited to try this new element of my ability again, then irritated that I wouldn't have even known I was capable of it if Zey hadn't barged into my life and ruined it. He sat in the chair near the now-dead fire, unmoving.

I dreamed of drowning in depthless black.

At some point in the early hours, my bladder refused to let me drift back to sleep after another bout of tossing and turning. I must've slept for a while though, because Zey was no longer in the chair. He was on his back on the bed next to me. I could just make out his faceless shape in the dark. I was a little concerned that he'd managed to get that close without me noticing.

I summoned a pair of thick socks to save my feet from the freezing stone floors and slipped out of the bed as silently as possible. I wasn't sure how sleep worked for Vuulectians, but maybe getting some would make him slightly more bearable to be around.

Maybe it was because I was half asleep or that the tiny windows of the cabin barely let in any light, but I didn't notice I was being stalked until it was too late.

My attacker grabbed me from behind and had me slammed against the wall next to the front door with a firm grip around my throat before I could say "surprise."

CHAPTER 8

The back of my skull smacked against the timber wall, making my ears ring, but reflexes kicked in, and I punched my attacker in the general rib area. My fist made a smacking sound, skin connecting with bare skin.

What in the naked ninja was happening?

My eyes adjusted to the dark, and his close proximity made me realize it was Zey pinning me to the wall, back in his chosen human form.

"Where are you going?" he growled as he grabbed my wrist with his free hand and slammed it above my head.

"To empty my bladder," I growled back. "What the fuck?"

"A likely excuse." His hand on my throat tightened, not enough to cut off air supply but enough to make me want to summon a weapon. I had to remind myself my blades and guns were useless.

"You will tell me which direction the Onuei are in right now. I will not allow you to try to take them for yourself.

They cannot be wielded by someone not of my realm, so your deception is pointless."

This motherfucker thought I was going after his trinkets for myself? *That's it.*

I summoned a zap. Now that I'd held one, it was easy enough to summon the closest one.

"Remove your hands immediately." I held the zap to his groin, my grip firm. Holding his gaze, I ignored the feeling of coarse hair brushing against my knuckles. This idiot really had sprung out of bed completely naked, thinking he was catching me in some grand plan to run away. Not to mention he'd gotten in the bed with me *completely naked*!

He lowered his gaze between our bodies, then looked at me with his eyes narrowed. Slowly, deliberately, he released his grip on my throat and wrist but stayed where he was, his body crowding mine.

"All I want is my life back so I can pretend I never met you in the first place. But if you want to try this on your own, have fun. My ability pulled me east. That's in that direction." I pointed to my right. "Now I'm going to pee and attempt to get some more sleep, *you paranoid son of a bitch.*"

I kept the zap in my grip and at the ready as I stared him down, telling him with my glare to back the fuck off.

"Perhaps . . ." He licked his lips and sighed, his warm breath washing over me. For some reason, I'd been expecting it to be cold. I shivered lightly, the cold wall at my back a sharp contrast to the warm body at my front.

"Perhaps my impatience and sense of urgency made me come to a hasty conclusion," Zey said, still not backing away from me—or the zap at his groin.

I eased the weapon back slightly but kept it at the ready. "The word you're looking for is *sorry.*"

He nodded. "I'm sorry that my concern for my entire

realm and sharing sensitive information with a person I hardly knew, in a world entirely new to me, made me somewhat suspicious."

"You don't sound sorry," I huffed, my chest brushing against his. Damn it! I wanted to hit him—or tase him—but that would surely draw attention. And why the hell was he still standing so close to me?

"Back off." I shoved his chest, and he barely moved. He gripped my wrist again, and I immediately pressed the zap to his groin.

His eyes narrowed, but he didn't look mad or worried. He looked amused.

"I know you can hit harder than that." He smiled.

"Yeah, well, I'm tired," I gritted out.

"And frustrated."

"You're in the room, so yeah."

He lowered his arm and mine, his hand still gripping my wrist.

"And tense."

"What's your point?" I intended for the words to come out biting, but they were more breathy than anything.

"As a solution to all of the above, and to show my sincere apology, I can offer you sexual gratification." He leaned in, his gaze fixed on me, but stopped with his lips a thin breath away from mine.

"What?" I blinked, trying to keep up with what the hell was happening. My bladder was no longer screaming at me and, at the mention of sexual anything, I realized that the focus had turned to other sensations in that same region.

"That is what you crave, isn't it? All the physiological signs are there." He brushed his cheek against mine, pressing his body flush against me. His naked, toned, strong body.

For a brief moment of insanity, my eyes fluttered closed, and I arched into him.

Then I came to my damn senses.

"No." I scrambled out from under him and took several steps back. I was mad at this infuriating, single-minded man. Screwing his brains out would *not* help the situation. Even if we were both into it, it would create more complications than it was worth. And he was into it—judging by the fully erect penis he was pointing at me.

"You can't just solve all your problems with sex, Zey!" I threw my hands up and headed to the bathroom, the zap still in a death grip in my hand.

I left him standing nude in the cold, dark cabin, and he was back in the chair by the fireplace by the time I came out of the bathroom.

I managed to get another few hours of fitful sleep but gave up trying around dawn. Sabrina brought us some breakfast and coffee, then drove us to a busy town further away from the village near Braemar Castle before anyone else was up and about.

"Just so you know," Sabrina said in the car as the trees zoomed past, clouded in fog. "The House of Spirit and Sapphire has sent word to all the other Houses overnight. There was no mention of a new portal, but they were very clear about wanting to find you and the fugitive you were aiding."

"Great." I sighed and wished we'd had time to stay a bit longer so I could dye my hair something less obvious. The hats would have to do.

"Why is this great?" Zey poked his head between the front seats, looking between us.

"Sarcasm, Zey," I said, pushing him back into his seat with a hand to the face.

Sabrina laughed silently. I could tell she had a million questions, but it was better for all of us if she knew as little as possible.

I wasn't much of a hugger, but I gave Sabrina a tight one when she dropped us off. She'd saved my ass, and I was starting to think we could be friends—if I survived this mess.

Zey and I went straight to the train station and waited for someone who looked like they were heading off for a long day at the office. It was the perfect time in the morning for it, so we didn't have to wait long. A guy in a business suit parked his unremarkable white sedan and trudged into the station. Summoning a magic detection spell packet, I performed the irritatingly complex procedure to make it work. A witch would've been able to tell with barely a wave of her hand, but I wasn't a witch, so expensive, complex spell packets it was! I made sure there was no tracking spell on the car, broke into it, and we got on the road.

I hated having to steal, but public transport was too risky. I'd make sure it was returned to him with a generous number of fae hairs in the glove compartment for his trouble.

Confident that the car wouldn't be reported stolen until late in the afternoon, we got on the road and headed east.

Once we were out of Death and Diamond territory, the drive was through No Man's Land for most of the way.

Zey was silent for the first hour, just looking out the window at the world passing us by. Of course, the peace didn't last.

"How much longer?" he asked.

I shrugged. "All I know is we're heading in the right general direction. I've never searched for something like this before, so it's hard to tell. Could be an hour, could be a day."

"A day?" he huffed.

"Don't get shitty with me!" I flashed him a reproachful look. "I don't make the rules. I'm doing my best here. I want this over with as soon as possible too—trust me."

He fell into silence again. And again, it didn't last long.

"What is that?" He pointed to a dilapidated, low building on the side of the road.

"A motel. They were common on Earth before House rule," I explained.

And that pretty much set the tone for the rest of the day. We stopped a few times so I could use the bathroom, refuel the car, and eat, and so Zey could drink water. Otherwise, we drove and drove and Zey asked question after question.

Why is everything split into territories?

What are the different Houses?

What happened during the Great Sacrifice?

What's a highway?

Why do you need to sleep so much?

At one point, we drove past an extremely faded billboard advertising an obsolete medication, and he asked what chlamydia was.

There was no pattern or clear connection between the things he was asking and only an occasional follow-up. I was happy to answer them all. It gave me something to do on the long drive other than glaring at the bastard and occasionally correcting our course as my connection to the Onuei strengthened.

Something occurred to me around mid-afternoon.

"What's with the questions?" I asked before he could fire another one. "You have that intuitive learning thing, don't you?"

"Yes, but I need at least some information to begin

with," he explained. "And I enjoy hearing your unique interpretation of the facts—your opinions, I believe you call them."

"You don't have opinions where you're from?" *What the fuck?*

"We do, they are just not so . . . colorful as yours. There is less nuance when everyone has the intuition to learn the truth of a situation—to an extent. Also, there is no sarcasm. I'm finding that I'm rather fond of it."

"You guys don't have sarcasm?" I gasped. "How do you express yourselves and crack jokes? It's downright barbaric. And here I was thinking you were more advanced as a species."

Zey chuckled and the look in his eyes was so *human*. He was adapting to Earth more and more by the minute.

It was late afternoon when we pulled into Liege thirteen hours later, in what used to be Belgium. I parked the car behind some buildings. The guy I'd stolen it from would've reported it missing when he got off the train a few hours earlier. It was time to ditch it.

I'd been feeling the Onuei more and more in the last hour, and I was pretty sure we were within walking distance. But I was starving, so I headed for the bustling strip of bars and food joints, present near any market in a No Man's Land area.

Limiting the amount of time I spent around people, I got a burger and fries to go, and Zey and I settled onto a park bench nearby. The burger was bland and the fries were stale, but I didn't care. It was food in my belly. I washed it down with Coke.

With a curious expression, Zey picked up the cup and smelled the straw. I watched him, finishing off the last of my burger. He wrapped his lips around the straw and frowned.

"How do you make the liquid come up?"

I chuckled and swallowed my massive mouthful of food. "You have to suck."

"Suck . . ."

I pursed my lips and demonstrated. He stared at my mouth as the furrow between his brows smoothed out. Then he put his mouth back on the straw and sucked hard. He must've got a massive mouthful . . . which he promptly sprayed out onto the grass.

"What is that?" He gave me a horrified look and gagged. "It's disgusting."

"Mostly cancer-causing chemicals and sugar." I laughed and summoned a bottle of water. "Here. This fixes everything."

He slammed it back in one go while I sipped on the Coke.

"Why do you consume that poison?" He looked genuinely aghast.

"We're self-destructive and hedonistic." I shrugged. "It's not a great combination."

"Is all human food so . . . toxic?"

"No. Just the cheap, fast stuff, usually. Do you have food where you're from? Or is it just water?"

"Some, but it is only consumed occasionally for pleasure. Water is all we need."

"What does it taste like? Is it—"

My questions were interrupted by a video call coming through on my phone, and I sprang to my feet. Zey was right there with me, shoulder against mine, tense and ready, even though he had no idea what made me react that way.

"It's OK." I pushed him away gently and stared at the incoming call with uncertainty.

"What is that?" he asked.

"It's a video call. From the looks of it, from a secure device. It's completely untraceable from either end," I explained. Electronic devices weren't really manufactured anymore, but the ones from before supes and Houses ruled the world were commonly spelled to work for our purposes. With an extra spell from a techno witch, they could even be made untraceable—by old-school tech and by magic. There was only one person I knew who would even bother to try to reach me securely.

"Can I have some privacy please? I need to have a conversation."

Zey looked at the phone in my hand, then back at me, his expression hardening. "No."

I ground my teeth. He still didn't trust me not to spill his secrets about his precious Onuei. Whatever.

I answered the video call. Lowell's head and shoulders appeared on the screen. My best friend's black hair was messy, his expression pinched and tired.

"Sky!" He sat up straighter. "Thank the gods. Are you OK?"

"Physically, yeah. Every other way . . ." I cringed. He mirrored the expression.

"Girl. The House of Spirit and Sapphire is in total chaos. I've never seen Reg this pissed off. What the hell is going on?"

He didn't ask where I was because he knew I would tell him if I could. That's why he'd made sure the call was untraceable before contacting me. No one would even know we spoke unless one of us told them.

"I'm not assisting a fugitive," I insisted. I felt a deep urge for someone to believe me, trust me when I spoke the truth. If my best friend didn't believe me, it was going to hurt. "I mean, I guess technically, we're both fugitives, but it's not like I had some massive plot to undermine the House or some shit. This is happening *to* me, and they all think I'm a traitor."

"Bunch of ungrateful assholes," Lowell grumbled and took a big gulp of his beer. "After all these years you busted your ass working for them. I don't know what the hell Reginald is thinking." Lowell was a bear shifter and had grown up in the House of Spirit and Sapphire. I was only a teenager when my mother died and I joined. Lowell and I had been friends from an early age. In a House with so many witches, complex rituals, and procedures, Lowell's massive build and natural affinity for physical things often left him overlooked and underappreciated. I was a mere human with a particularly handy ability. We'd both had to fight to prove we belonged in our House.

"It doesn't matter." I smiled, surprised at how difficult it was to swallow around the lump in my throat. The relief at his outrage on my behalf was palpable. "*You* don't think I'm the bad guy with some shady plan, and that's all that matters." I was running around with a guy from another realm, hiding from everyone, so of course getting my life and my reputation back mattered. But in that moment, I only cared what my bestie thought. I hadn't realized how badly I just wanted to have someone on my side.

"As if you could keep a secret from me," Lowell scoffed. "Especially one this big."

"Right?! Can you please go tell those assholes that if I had some evil plot against them, you would've known?"

"I have. Why do you think I hadn't called until now? They've been questioning me and watching my every move since you portaled out of Melbourne." He sighed, then took a chug of beer and clapped his hands. "Right! So, what's the plan? What can I do?"

I was acutely aware of Zey standing just a few feet away, watching and listening closely. I knew he didn't want me to share any information with anyone, but he could go suck it.

"I love you for offering, but all you can do is stay safe and tell no one you spoke to me. The last thing I need right now is to worry about you being hurt or excommunicated because of me."

"Really?" He deflated. "Sky, I know you're an independent, strong woman and all that, but come on. You don't have to do everything on your own."

"I'm not on my own." I threw an exasperated look at Zey. "Unfortunately . . ."

"Right." Lowell followed my gaze like he could look through the phone and see what I was glaring it. "Who is this 'individual' you're in cahoots with."

"I'm still trying to figure that out, but I'm trying to help him find something." Zey stepped closer, looking like he was ready to slap a hand over my mouth. I ignored him. "When we find what we're looking for, he's going to help me clear this mess up. Everything's going to be fine." I really, really hoped that was true.

Lowell's image wavered; the call tracing protection spell was running out.

"Shit." He took a deep breath. "I'm not sure how much longer we have."

"It's OK. Thank you for calling. You have no idea how much this means to me."

He smiled and, at the last moment, I thought of something.

"Lowell, there might be something you can do to help," I rushed out.

He nodded and leaned forward. "Hurry."

The phone flickered again. Zey might be pissed at what I was about to tell Lowell, but he'd just have to deal with it.

"Zey is from another realm—a totally new realm." Zey gave me a what-the-fuck look but didn't lunge for me. Lowell stared at me in shock. "A new portal opened in Melbourne a few days ago. I don't know why the House is keeping it secret, but if you can leak the info to the other Houses—safely—that would help us."

He nodded and I could see the million questions floating in his eyes. "I'll do my best."

The call ended and my friend's face disappeared. I sank onto the hard bench and dropped my head into my hands. I didn't even get to say bye, but I was grateful to have been able to speak to him.

"It was important to you—to have this friend believe you," Zey said, sitting down beside me.

"Yes," I sighed and sat up. I was a little surprised that he was leading with that and not grabbing me by the throat to demand why I was spilling his realm's secrets. "Why do you care?"

He didn't answer. After a beat, he asked, "Why would it help us for more people to know about the portal?"

I answered his question with a question. "What was it like in your realm when the portals started appearing?"

"Exciting, frightening. It was all anyone could talk about." Realization settled in and he gave me a small smile. I nodded.

"I don't know why my House is keeping it secret, although I'd hazard a guess it has something to do with getting the upper hand on the other Houses. Power is everything in this world. Anyway, if word gets out there's a new portal with a previously unknown species on the other side, it will be a pretty damn good distraction. The Houses will have their hands full trying to figure out more information, the House of Spirit and Sapphire will be busy defending their decision to keep it a secret, and the public will be just as obsessed with the development as your people were."

"And we can focus on our search in the chaos." He looked me up and down, like he was seeing me for the first time. "Clever."

"Come on. Let's fetch the first Onuei. It should be within walking distance now." I stood and started walking in the direction that my ability was pulling me. I wasn't sure if I was pleased that he thought I was clever or pissed that it seemed to come as a surprise to him. I also wasn't sure why I cared.

CHAPTER 9

My seeking ability led us to the local dump. We walked for about an hour to reach it, and it was fully dark by the time we got to the locked gates.

I dragged a hand down my face. I couldn't believe I had to dig through literal trash to find Zey's precious. The smell was already making me gag.

"What is this place?" Zey asked, his face screwed up in disgust.

"This is where the Onuei is hiding." There was no use delaying the inevitable. I pulled up the bottom of the chain-link fence gate and squeezed through, then held it for Zey. I wasn't worried about any magical wards on this gate—it was highly unlikely anyone would bother to spend money on protecting a place most people avoided anyway.

The few streetlamps barely illuminated the area a few feet in. I summoned a flashlight and closed my eyes to pinpoint a direction. The smell was distracting and made it impossible to take deep, centering breaths. Then it started to rain, and I was thoroughly distracted. I huffed, irritated.

Next to me, Zey seemed to have no trouble finding Zen. He had a serene look on his face as he stood there, his face tipped up to the sky, his eyes closed. The rain was a light sprinkle, and I couldn't seem to take my eyes off the strong lines of his features as water gathered all over his skin. He did that mesmerizing rippling thing, the depthless black flowing in waves over his skin. He let the droplets linger before absorbing them.

After a long moment, he opened his eyes and looked at me.

"Which way, seeker?" he asked.

I cleared my throat. "I'm struggling to focus. Give me a moment."

He took my hand and held it firmly. I glanced down, then back into his eyes.

"What are you doing?" I asked.

"It helps when you touch me, right? It's easier for you to find the Onuei?"

"Right. Yeah, good. OK." Ignoring the weirdness, I forced myself to focus. The ribbons unfurled like tendrils in my mind, showing me a path through the mounds of trash.

Zey started rubbing small circles against the back of my hand with his thumb. For a few seconds, I held off telling him which direction we needed to take. The sensation was more comforting than I cared to admit, and I couldn't stop myself from enjoying it for just a little bit.

"This way," I said, finally dropping his hand and taking the lead.

We wove through the piles of trash, some of them so high that my flashlight beam couldn't reach the top. The rain continued to fall gently but steadily, soaking through my clothes bit by bit.

Eventually, the ribbons in my mind floated off the

pathway and into a pile of metal scraps. There was every-thing from bits of wire to the carcasses of old cars. It looked like a death trap.

"OK, your turn." I pointed into the mess of murderous metal. "Seeing as you can't die from being impaled by a rusty steel rod and I can, you can climb into that and fetch your Onuei."

Zey started climbing over the mess before I even finished speaking. Several times, sharp metal pierced his skin as he scrambled over it all. I cringed every time, but he didn't even seem to notice. It just passed through him like a hot knife through butter. Like a hot metal beam through a butter-man. An image of Zey standing before me, his body made entirely of butter flashed through my mind. I snorted.

"What is it?" He called from somewhere within the metal heap.

"Nothing," I called back. "Do you need me to tell you where to look?"

"No. I can feel the energy of the Onuei now."

With nothing better to do, I swung the flashlight around, gawking at all the crap piles while I waited. There was a section of building materials, like bricks and pavers, piled high like the metal, as well as an area with green waste. Piles of branches sat next to a woodchipper. I guessed this was part of the dump where they sorted what was salvageable.

Zey grunted and I turned the beam of light onto him in time to see him stumble out of the pile of metal. He righted himself as a few loose bits clanged off the mound.

"Did you get it?" I asked.

He grinned and held his hand out to show me what he had clutched in it.

"Uh . . ." I bit my lip, trying not to laugh. "That's a hand crank . . . I think." I was pretty sure that was what they were called; there were very few non-electric vehicles left. "A long time ago, it was used to manually wind down the windows in a car."

"This is the Onuei," he said with unwavering certainty. "When they passed through the portal, they scattered, and their magic disguised them to keep them hidden until the one truly worthy to lead came for them."

I wiped the rain out of my eyes and tapped into my power. Sure enough, the ribbons in my mind wound around the black piece of plastic junk in Zey's hand.

"Whatever. Let's get out of this rain." I started walking back the way we'd come. It would've been good to have a visual—it would make finding the other two Onuei easier—but I was quickly learning that nothing was easy with Zey.

I'd barely taken a few steps when he gripped my upper arm firmly and leaned in close.

"They found us," he said, staring into the darkness off to his left.

See? No such thing as easy with this guy.

"Maybe there's another way out." I spun on my heel and started marching in the opposite direction to where he was looking.

"Too late," Zey gritted out as he yanked me behind a forklift. I dropped the flashlight. Something thunked into the vehicle, and a spark of electricity lit up the area for a split second.

Muttering every curse in English that I knew, and a few in other languages, I summoned the zap that had hit the forklift. I sprang up, found the nearest Vuulectian, and threw it. I got him in the shoulder.

The flashlight was on the ground, illuminating the rain that continued to fall steadily and all the black shapes closing in. There was no one around, so the Vuulectians hadn't bothered with shifting into human forms. They stalked forward with their inky black bodies and faceless heads.

"Holy shit! How many are there?" I ducked back down. There were way more of them than the group of about a dozen that I'd seen in Melbourne.

"Forty-six," Zey stated matter-of-factly. Fuck. We couldn't take that many. "Summon more zaps," he ordered. Ignoring the irritation at his tone, I did exactly that. Because it was the best way to fight them—not because Zey told me to.

I sent my power out, the ribbons snapping through space and splitting in many different directions. I yanked the closest one and handed it to Zey, then immediately summoned another. He stood and threw it, reaching for another without even looking.

Using the forklift as cover, we fell into a rhythm. I summoned zap after zap, handing them to Zey, who fired them off like a machine. He knew the best way to wield them and the best spots to hit to incapacitate his buddies. Sometimes, I summoned the things right out of the hands of a Vuulectian about to throw one.

It had them confused for a while, but they quickly figured out what I was doing and changed tactics. While most of them continued the barrage of zaps, keeping us busy and focused on them, a few were trying to get closer to us unnoticed. We were ducking the zaps left, right, and center. A few had grazed us each, but thankfully hadn't done massive damage. Zey recovered quickly with the easy access to water since it was falling from the sky. But so did the others.

We were both tiring. And there were so many of them.

Before I could think of some creative way out of this situation, one of the Vuulectians took me by surprise. It appeared next to me, having darted around the forklift without me noticing. I ducked as it lunged for me, but not fast enough. It caught me on the side of the head, making my ears ring for a moment. I pushed through it and kicked out, my heavy boot connecting with its side. It lunged for me again. I summoned a zap and jammed it into the side of its head. The Vuulectian went down immediately, twitching, those ripples jerking over its skin.

Another two replaced it. Grunting and snarling like an animal, I threw punches and kicks. I summoned another zap, but there were two of them, and I couldn't pin one down to get it with my weapon.

"Zey!" I barked. "A little help here?"

One of them got behind me and grabbed my elbows as the other lunged for my front. I leaned all my weight back, lifted my legs, and kicked it in the chest. It fell backwards and landed in a puddle. I managed to stab the zap into the leg of the one behind me and punched it in its faceless mug —hard.

I whirled around and saw why Zey hadn't come to my aid. He was struggling with three of his own buddies. None of them had zaps, so they were fighting it out the good old-fashioned way. They moved fluidly but with impressive speed, their limbs reminding me of dancers as they arced through the air elegantly, flicking rain as they moved.

Zey was truly a warrior. He'd stayed in his human form but moved with just as much grace and flow as the rest of them. He was clearly more skilled and experienced, managing to hold three of them off on his own.

I summoned a zap and threw it at the back of a Vuulectian. His back arched and he sank to his knees, trying to reach the thing awkwardly. I summoned another as I ran towards them. Zey yanked the zap out of the first one's back as he kicked another in the stomach, sending him stumbling towards me. I stabbed him in the side of the head, and he went down. The head thing seemed to work best, and I was sticking to it. Zey used the zap he had to incapacitate the other two.

"Run," I rushed out, panting.

He shook his head. "They're all around."

"Why aren't they coming for us?" I peeked around the forklift as Zey did the same on the other side. Vuulectians were all around, some still unconscious, some slowly getting back up and helping their buddies. The rain continued to fall, providing them with a constant stream of recharge juice.

It was a good opportunity to escape. Why was Zey not listening to me?

I caught a glimpse of movement in the light of the flashlight, and it clicked into place. The ones who were still unhurt, or who had recovered, were using the piles of trash as cover, trying to get to us stealthily.

I started summoning zaps, as many as I could, handing them to Zey and tucking them into my pockets and waistband. We moved so we were back-to-back. My chest heaved and my muscles screamed in protest. I had no idea what we could possibly do to get out of this, but I was so far past the point of problem solving. I was acting on pure instinct, ready to fight until I couldn't any longer.

When they made their move, it was fast and synchronized. They swarmed us from all sides. Zey and I fought like caged animals, throwing zaps and punches and kicks, but it was only a matter of minutes before we were overwhelmed and separated.

They tackled Zey to the ground, and the Onuei went flying through the air. It landed in front of the flashlight, looking like a useless piece of junk as chaos reigned all around. With a renewed burst of determination, Zey managed to break free.

A Vuulectian came at me, and I used my last zap to bring him down. I didn't see the other one coming. It rushed me from the darkness, and pain exploded in my thigh. Bastard had stabbed me with a broken pipe.

I screamed, the guttural sound cutting through the silence, drowning out the sound of rain pelting the sodden ground.

CHAPTER 10

All the Vuulectians froze for a beat and looked in my direction, and I realized none of them had made any noise this whole time.

My eyes fixed on Zey, and it felt like time slowed for a brief moment as I fell, my leg no longer able to hold my weight. He took in what was happening to me, everyone else's momentary distraction. I may have caught a brief look of uncertainty in his gaze, but I was pretty sure it was just my desperation that conjured it.

He lunged for the Onuei, leaving me at the mercy of one of his buddies. The broken pipe came down on my head, and I dropped. When my face landed in the water-logged gravel, I stayed down. The pipe clattered to the ground next to me, my assailant apparently having decided I was no longer a threat.

My vision wavered. All the Vuulectians were after Zey now. Served him right for not even trying to help me. Stupid shapeshifting shithead.

I was so done with all of this crap.

My eyes landed on a portable spotlight nearby, and I

pushed myself up. It was one of those big lights on wheels, at least eight feet tall. I dragged myself over to it, my leg screaming in protest. I gritted my teeth against the pain and pulled myself up by sheer force of will. I had to make sure the rubber soles of my boots were planted on the ground.

Putting all my weight on my good leg, I found the switch and turned the thing on. It was so bright in the darkness it hurt my eyes.

Everyone stopped what they were doing and turned towards me. I wasn't sure where Zey was, but he could fry with the rest of them for all I cared.

I was sure I looked maniacal as I grinned at them. With one hand I gave them all the middle finger, and with the other I summoned a gun. I shot at the light where it was joined to the base. Those things were designed not to tip, so I fired shot after shot until it separated from the base and started to teeter. The light flickered. I gave it a shove with my shoulder, and it crashed into the water-logged ground. The spotlight went out, and sparks went flying as electricity zapped through the water.

All the Vuulectians stiffened and fell, twitching on the ground as the current passed through the water. I slumped against a pile of timber, careful to avoid anything metal.

"I think you got them all." Zey's voice cut through the relative silence. "You can turn it off now."

"Not all of them!" I yelled back. "You're still standing."

I couldn't see him. Wherever he was hiding from the electric current, he sounded close, but he was obscured by the garbage and the darkness. The sound of the rain was the only thing I could hear now, that and my own labored breathing.

"Sky?" Zey sounded uncertain. "You're going to kill them if you don't turn that off soon."

I huffed and reached down, flipping the switch off. The hum of electricity died.

"What do you care?" It would make our lives easier if they all died, but I didn't really want to add 'mass murderer' to my growing list of unsavory titles.

There was a splash in the distance and then the crunch of gravel under feet. Zey came around from behind a pile of tires.

"Because life is sacred," he said. "They may be going against what is good and right about our people and our way of life, but they are still Vuulectians, still living beings. We do not kill."

I raised my gun and shot him in the head.

The bullet made his head jerk back. He gave me a deep frown before spitting it out to the side.

"That's for letting me get stabbed with a rusty pipe." I glared at him.

He stopped right in front of me and ground his teeth, looking like he was reconsidering his no-killing rule.

"I couldn't let them get the Onuei," he said, clearly forcing a calm tone. Like I was the one being unreasonable.

"Ugh! Whatever." I hobbled around him and started dragging my soggy, bleeding, tired ass towards the exit. It was slow going and every step was agony.

I heard Zey's footsteps catching up behind me, but I still nearly shot him again when he knocked my feet out from under me. I hadn't been expecting it, and I certainly hadn't been expecting not to eat gravel. Instead, I found myself in his arms.

"What the fuck are you doing?" I wrapped my arms around his neck to steady myself. It felt good to be off my injured leg, but it still hurt when I got jostled.

Zey stared straight ahead, setting a fast pace. "It will

take them a long time to recover, but we still need to be as far away as possible when they do. Preferably on the other side of a body of water."

I wanted to argue, to demand he put me down. But I wasn't going to get far on my own, and I was freezing from all the rain. It felt nice to have his warmth seep through the drenched clothing. There was no way in hell I'd ever tell him he was right though, so I just kept my mouth shut and let him carry me to the exit.

The rain started to ease up as we walked out of the now busted gate—a resounding end to the violence behind us.

With the threat removed, the adrenaline drained from my body, and I started to feel every ache and pain as shivers shook my bones. I summoned a thick bandage and pressed it against my wound as hard as I could handle. It would have to do until we could get somewhere safe. I also summoned a potion that would dull the pain and downed the horribly bitter liquid in one go. I should've stocked up on healing potions or vampire saliva with my last pay. But I'd been in meetings in the safety of our House zone and hadn't been expecting to be sent on any dangerous missions.

Zey carried me for the hour it took to walk back to the nearest town. He didn't slow his pace, didn't struggle with my weight, didn't even breathe heavily.

We "borrowed" a car that was parked behind the bar where I'd purchased my food earlier. I was not confident in Zey's ability to drive, but I was in no state to do it myself.

I leaned my head on the window and closed my eyes. When I opened them again, we were crossing a bridge. It was still dark, but I assumed there was a river flowing below.

"We should cross a few rivers if we can." My voice was

hoarse. I reached for my cell, hoping it had survived the drenching and fighting. "I'll have a look at a map to see—"

Zey placed a gentle hand on mine, stopping my search and my words. "We have crossed three bodies of water already."

Shit. How long was I out?

"OK, then. Then we should . . . um . . ."

"Find somewhere safe so you can rest and tend to your wound?" He glanced at me and frowned. "It is still leaking blood."

"Yeah. Human bodies tend to leak blood when they're punctured." I intended for it to sound sarcastic and accusing, but it just came out sounding weak. Shit. Maybe I *was* losing too much blood.

"Do you have another friend nearby who can assist us?"

"No. I hardly have any friends," I mumbled, then pointed to an upcoming turn. "Turn here and follow those signs."

For once, Zey did as he was told, pulling into a motel just off the main road. He parked in a dark corner of the lot as I summoned some vials. I closed my eyes and lost another chunk of time, waking to him opening my door and lifting me out.

Apparently, he'd got us a room, and before I knew what was happening, he carried me into it. He went to place me on one of the two queen beds.

"No, no." I pointed to the only other door in the beige and green room, faintly lit by one crooked lamp. "Bathroom."

He changed direction and took me into the bathroom, depositing me on the edge of the tub. I winced when he turned the light on, but it helped to rouse me a little.

A trail of blood led out the door. Not good.

I summoned a first aid kit, then peeled my soaking wet jacket and top off my aching body. Zey stood in the corner and watched me struggle to balance while I undressed. I nearly fell backwards into the tub as I tried to pull my pants down, but he shot forward and caught me.

Wordlessly he pulled me to my feet and crouched down. I held on to his shoulders, whimpering as he peeled the pants over my injury. He helped me out of the pants, boots, and socks, then left me standing there as he turned on his heel and left the room.

OK, then. Fine. Whatever. Wouldn't be the first time I had to patch myself up.

He returned a moment later with one of the two chairs that were tucked under the little table next to the door. Placing it in the middle of the bathroom, he guided me down into the seat.

"How do I make it stop leaking?" he asked, crouching down next to me. I finally took a proper look. There was a jagged, deep gouge in the side of my upper thigh. The bleeding was slowing down, but the fact it was still bleeding after all this time told me it was *deep*. It was a good thing the bastard got me in a fleshy part—I didn't think it had reached bone.

"We need to clean it first." I gestured to the first aid kit, and Zey opened it. "The antiseptic. The wound has to be disinfected, then bandaged." It probably needed stitches too, but I was too wrecked to deal with that. Hopefully, I'd find some way to get my hands on a healing potion or some vampire saliva tomorrow.

Zey got to work, focused on what he was doing. His intuitive learning must've filled in the basics of wound care, because I sat in silence while he worked. Well, unless you counted the stream of curses I let loose when he poured the antiseptic all over my leg.

"Thanks," I said as he finished securing the bandage. "For carrying me all that way, and for this." I gestured to my leg.

He looked up at me with those unusual eyes, and I felt like he was studying me again, trying to figure something out about the species.

"I am . . . pleased that you are not dead," he said, his gaze intense. Mirth bubbled up my chest at his strange choice of words, but it died as quickly as it came. I was suddenly acutely aware of his hand on my thigh. It was close to the bandage, his thumb rubbing back and forth in miniscule motions. I wasn't even sure he was aware he was doing it.

He was at about eye level, kneeling in front of me. He lifted his other arm and gripped the back of the chair. I leaned into him reflexively. He'd carried me in his arms away from danger, he'd figured out how to drive and how to reserve a motel room to get us somewhere safe, he'd cleaned and bandaged my wound . . . he was pleased I wasn't dead.

And with his arms where they were, I felt safe in the cocoon of the moment.

Zey tracked my movement and mirrored it until we were nose-to-nose, staring into each other's eyes like if we just looked hard enough, long enough, we'd be able to figure out the answers for all the messy questions we had about our situation.

He licked his lips. I parted mine on an exhale as pressure built low in my belly. Anticipation made my skin tingly. He rubbed his nose against mine, tilting his head. I released a tiny, involuntary moan as I closed my eyes and—

No!

I shoved him back and leaned away.

It was his fault I had a wound that needed bandaging in the first place. It was his fault my life was a total fucking mess. He was only pleased his buddies hadn't offed me because he needed me to find his other two trinkets. Whatever this rush of lust was, it was just a response to an intense situation.

"Sky?" His fingers flexed on my thigh.

"I need to sleep," I said, gripping the edge of the sink to pull myself up.

"Of course." He wrapped an arm around my back and leaned down to pick me up.

"No!" I slapped at his shoulder and arm until he backed up, giving me a perplexed, displeased look. "I can do it myself," I stated and forced myself to turn away from him. I thought I caught a glimpse of hurt in that beautiful face that was getting more expressive every day, but I must've been hallucinating.

I hobbled over to the nearest bed and peeled my still-wet bra and underwear off before getting under the covers. I could feel his eyes on me for a long moment before the bathroom door clicked shut, but I was already falling asleep.

CHAPTER 11

I woke slowly, rubbing my face against the thin, scratchy pillowcase. I didn't want to move out of the cheap-but-warm sheets, but I knew I couldn't sleep away the day—as much as my body needed it. We had to keep moving; I needed to search for the next Onuei. I had to get my hands on something healing first though. We weren't going to get far with me injured like I was.

A plan beginning to form in my mind, I blinked my eyes open slowly. Zey was sitting on the bed directly opposite, facing me, his hands in his lap.

I didn't expect him to be so close, and I startled. Pain shot through my leg at the sudden movement, and I winced.

"What the fuck, dude?" I sat up glaring at him. "Were you watching me sleep?"

"Yes," he said, his gaze dropping to my chest for a brief second.

Remembering that I'd gone to sleep completely naked, I grabbed the edge of the blanket to cover myself up. But then I stopped myself and threw it completely off. If he was so unbothered by nudity, then I wasn't going to make myself uncomfortable around him. More uncomfortable than I already was that is . . . and irritated.

"I know you don't have eyes where you're from, but here, it's rude to stare," I said, twisting to look at my bandage. "And it's creepy to watch people sleep."

"There was nothing else to do, and I didn't want to disturb you. Your dressing needs to be changed."

"Yeah, I know." I rubbed my eye with the heel of my hand and moved to get up. Zey got to his feet and stopped me with a gentle touch to my shoulder. He pushed me back down to the pillow and sat next to me, first aid kit in hand. Silently, he cleaned the wound and changed the dressing. I just lay there, feeling all conflicted and shit. Why did he have to be so matter-of-factly attentive when he was the literal bane of my existence. It really wasn't fair that he wasn't affected by my body laid out in front of him. Like *at all*. I guessed hormones weren't a thing either where he was from. Did they even have sex? How did they reproduce?

"Your wound is infected. We need to get some antibiotics," he stated as he finished.

"It looks fine." I frowned. There was no pus or any other signs of infection.

"I can sense it. In your blood." He looked down at my leg, at the spot where his hand was resting just below my wound. His brow furrowed, like the infection had personally offended him.

I brushed his hand away and got out of bed on the opposite side.

"I'll get something better than antibiotics and be ready to search for the next Onuei by the end of the day. No need to get worked up about it," I said as I walked to the bathroom with my shoulders back.

After a quick shower, I summoned myself a change of

clothes, put my hair up in a braid, and walked out to find Zey sitting in one of the chairs at the little table. The second one was back in its spot, my dry blood blending in with the dark fabric of the seat. A paper bag and a takeout cup sat on the table.

I hobbled over, Zey watching my every move.

"What's this?" I frowned.

"You require sustenance, do you not?" He cocked his head to the side, his expression unreadable.

"I . . . yes. You went out to get me breakfast? Were you careful not to be seen?"

"Of course." He gave me a small, amused smile as he shifted only his face into that of an older man with bushy eyebrows, then returned it back to his own.

I lowered myself gingerly onto the chair and dug into the bacon and egg bagel. I was starving. The cup was full of steaming coffee with just a splash of cream and half a sugar. He knew exactly how I had my coffee.

"Thank you." I avoided his gaze as I took a big bite of the bagel.

"It's my pleasure," he replied, and I could feel his eyes boring into my skull. I focused intently on finishing my breakfast.

"Sky." He reached across the table, as if to take my hand, but drew it back. "We don't—"

"Have a lot of time." I put my big-girl pants on and looked at him. He'd patched me up, fed and watered me, and now he wanted me to do my job. "I know."

"That's not . . ." He frowned, then leaned back, looking at me like my human needs were beyond inconvenient. "Where do we get what you need to heal?"

He wasn't going to like it, but whether I went for a healing spell or vamp saliva, I needed to rest while it did its thing. It would take a fraction of the time a wound like this took to heal naturally—maybe half a day or so—but it was time we could scarcely afford to lose.

He should've thought of that before letting me get stabbed.

"From someone who owes me a favor," I said, sipping on my coffee. "Where's the Onuei?"

"Why?" His eyes narrowed.

I rolled mine. "If I hold it, it should be easier for me to find the next one. I'll need some time to heal when I get what I need to fix this." I huffed and gestured to my leg. "I'd rather make sure where we go to get it is not in the opposite direction of the closest Onuei. I promise not to use it to try to take over the world."

Zey sighed and shook his head, then pulled the crank out of his pocket. I set the coffee down and reached for it, but he held on to it when I tried to take it.

"Seriously?"

"Are you sure you're well enough to do this now? Perhaps we should get you healed first."

I yanked the black plastic from his grip. "Stop telling me how to do my job."

Ignoring his disapproving glare, I closed my eyes and tuned in to the energy of the Onuei. I'd searched for magical items before, even summoned them, so I was used to the extra layer of energy that came with them. It was a kind of hum, more alive than a regular inanimate object. But I'd never felt something like this. It had been muted when I used Zey as a conduit to search for them, and I'd dismissed it as that same magical item hum I was used to. Now that I held one in my hands, could sense the full force of its energy, I knew this was unlike anything I'd seen before. It was difficult to describe, but it was . . . *deep* was the best word I could come up with.

To my relief, holding the Onuei definitely helped me pick up on the next closest one. The ribbons in my mind were much less frayed and brittle than they had been last time. I got a very clear sense that we needed to head to Brazil, which meant we needed a powerful witch to open a portal. But first, I needed something to heal this wound.

I knew a vampire not too far from where we were who owed me a favor. I just hoped he could help us with both problems, because I had no vamp saliva in my storage, and I didn't know any witches in this part of Europe.

I instructed Zey on how to buy a car, showed him a picture of the most average man I could find on the internet, summoned a wad of angel feathers, and sent him out to get us a ride.

He came back an hour later with a much newer model than I'd expected, and we got on the road.

It had been very late when we checked into the motel, and I'd slept for a long time, so it was late afternoon by the time we took to the road. I let him drive, my injury making it difficult to do much of anything.

I wished he'd go faster, but he stuck to a sensible, steady speed. I just wanted to get better as soon as possible. I hated feeling weak, having to rely on others. I prided myself on being able to take care of my damn self. I'd been strong and independent since I was a teenager. It was hard to survive in this world if you weren't.

My phone vibrated, and I pulled it from my pocket to find a message from an unknown contact. When I saw the contents, I was pretty sure it was Lowell giving me a heads up.

It was a report about a new portal that had opened in

Melbourne. Apparently, representatives from the House of Spirit and Sapphire had made contact with our new friends and were communicating amicably with the new species. The report ended with a description of me and Zey, stating we were very dangerous and in the Liege area. It had been sent to all House leaders.

I read it to Zey, and we exchanged a look. Only the Vuulectians had seen us at the dump. They were clearly sharing information with my House. But why? What did the House of Spirit and Sapphire get out of the deal?

"Looks like your buddies and my buddies have come to an agreement," I said.

"It would certainly appear so." Zey's hands tightened on the steering wheel. "I suspected as much when Silovi was threatening us at the place with all the trash, but I wondered if it was an empty threat."

"The dump," I reflexively supplied. "Wait, who's Sil-whatever? Someone spoke to you?"

"Silovisuvinoucraptiles. They are one of the leaders of Lineg Legion. They were all throwing insults and threats at us the whole time. You didn't hear it?"

"No! I think I would've remembered that."

"Oh. We communicated in our usual way." He tapped the side of his head. "I guess we didn't account for the different frequency of your mind in the mess of the situation."

"Rude." I crossed my arms.

Zey's lips twitched into a brief, amused smile. "Silovi said that they had Vuulectians in every major city, that they would find the Onuei faster than I ever could alone, and I should just give up and join them. They also said rude things about you."

"Me?" I pressed a hand to my chest, outraged. "Like

119

what? Never mind. I don't care. That only confirms that they're working with the House of Spirit and Sapphire. No way they could get that many through a portal unnoticed, and they'd definitely need help to get to other parts of the world so fast."

Zey hummed but kept his eyes on the road. He looked disturbed.

"Are you worried they will get to the Onuei first?" I asked.

"Yes. The more of them there are, the easier they will be able to sense the energy—just like how they find me."

"Is that why you were able to feel the Onuei in the pile of metal once we got close to it?"

"Yes, but only because we were so close."

"How did you think you were going to find them on your own?" He'd come charging over here on an impossible mission with absolutely no knowledge of the realm he was stepping into. I had to hand it to him—it was ballsy.

"I didn't exactly have a plan. I was running for my life, and I knew I had to follow the Onuei."

"Lucky I was the one that found you then." I looked out the window. We were getting close.

"Yes. Lucky." Zey kept his eyes glued to the road, but there was something in his expression, in the set of his jaw— something . . . more.

I didn't have time to worry about it, and I told him where to turn and park.

It was evening when we reached the No Man's Land town in the German countryside, and it was a cold one. There weren't many people about on the residential street, but apartment buildings were busy, and the Houseless were desperate. I hoped the dark would be enough cover for us to get from the car into the safety of the apartment on the eighth floor.

Acutely aware of the ache in my leg and the time pressure, I didn't wait to get moving. Zey helped me out of the car, through the building, and up to the eighth floor. I leaned on him more than I wanted to. And I was starting to feel a bit feverish. Maybe he was right about that infection.

We stopped in front of one of the many identical doors in the hallway. I knocked. We waited for only a few moments before it swung open.

Mark's youthful face drained of color when he saw me on the other side of the door. And that was a feat, considering he was Ethiopian, and a vampire.

"No," he gasped, and slammed the door in my face.

"Absolutely not," he called through the door. "Go away!"

CHAPTER 12

I knocked lightly on the door again.

"You owe me, Mark," I said barely above a whisper, knowing he'd hear me perfectly with his vamp hearing.

After a few silent moments, the door opened once again. Mark glared at me as he stepped back and aggressively gestured for us to come inside. He poked his head out and looked up and down the corridor before closing it.

"You couldn't have called in your favor when you weren't literally the most wanted person on the planet?" He folded his arms, still glaring. He had a good glare on him. Very expressive, ten out of ten intensity.

"Haven't needed a favor this big until now." I shrugged.

"You're a bitch."

"Never said I wasn't."

"Mark." Another man's voice came from somewhere in the apartment, followed by soft footfalls. "Do you think we have enough Jell-O shots?"

Zey stepped forward slightly, as if to shield me with his body.

"Hey, Mitch." I flashed Mark's human husband a grin. Mark chose to live in No Man's Land without the protection of a House because he'd fallen in love—with a human. No House would take Mitch, so they'd built a life in one of the tamer parts of No Man's Land.

"Sky!" His eyes went wide, and he slapped a hand over his mouth. Unlike Mark, Mitch didn't try to make me leave. He rushed forward and wrapped me up in a hug. "Everyone is talking about you."

"Yeah, I know."

"Just tell us what you want and leave," Mark grumbled. Mitch smacked him on the chest.

"We owe her big time. Drop the attitude, old man."

"Yeah, take the stick out of your ass and help an old friend." I winced as I put too much weight on my leg.

Zey leaned his head to the side and frowned, trying to see if Mark really had a stick protruding from his butt.

"Sky, he looks rather youthful," Zey said, clearly confused.

Mitch burst out laughing.

"Yeah. Mark is a vampire. One hundred forty-two years old and perpetually stuck looking like a twenty-something." I chuckled.

It was like a lightbulb went off in his head when I said vampire. "Sky requires your saliva."

Like I was trying to drive the point home, my vision blurred, and I swayed on the spot. Zey supported me with an arm around my waist as I sagged against him.

I blacked out for a moment, and next thing I knew, Zey was carrying me through the apartment as Mark and Mitch spoke in urgent voices.

Then I was being lowered to a bed, unable to stifle a groan of pain from my leg being jostled.

Finally, gentle hands removed my pants, and I sighed in relief at the cool sensation of vampire saliva being spread onto my aching wound.

The next time I woke, it was with a start. I heard glass smashing and jolted into a sitting position, summoning my favorite fighting knife all in the same breath.

Zey's hand reached out slowly. He placed it over my tense fist and guided me to lower the blade as I took in my surroundings.

"You're safe," he said. And he was right. We were in a bedroom—a spare bedroom if the mishmash of leftover furniture was anything to go by. The bed didn't match the side tables, and there were no personal touches. I remembered coming to Mark and Mitch's place, but the rest was a bit of a blur.

"I heard glass smashing," I said, lowering the knife. My voice sounded hoarse and came out as barely a whisper.

Zey glanced up from his spot on the floor and placed his finger to his lips. *"You must be silent."* His voice rang clear in my head. *"Your friends are having a party. There are some vampires present, two shifters, a fae, and many humans. Most of the people are inebriated, and there is much noise, but we must still be silent."*

He lowered his gaze down to my leg as he spoke. He was sitting right next to the bed, his face level with my wound. I was pantsless, only in my underwear and the T-shirt I'd had on under my jacket. Did he undress me? I suppose if they needed to check the wound . . .

And why were the boys having a party right now? Didn't they know how dangerous this was for all of us? Although, if it had been planned already, it would've looked more suspicious to cancel it. Most of the people present wouldn't be affiliated with a House, but some might. Plus handing over two wanted fugitives could be leverage to get yourself *into* a House if you'd previously failed.

I tapped Zey on the head to get his attention, then gestured to his position and gave him a "WTF are you doing" look.

He answered in my mind, of course. *"I was watching you sleep."*

I raised an eyebrow and pursed my lips. His mouth slowly curved into a smirk and his eyes sparkled, making his already annoyingly stunning features even more striking.

Was he teasing me? And when did he learn how to smirk?

He rose silently and sat on the bed, facing me.

"I was watching your wound heal," he explained. *"And tracking the infection. It is all clear now. And your flesh is nearly back to its previous unblemished state."*

We both reached for the spot on my leg at the same time. Any normal person would've pulled their hand back, but Zey wasn't normal. Was he even a person as we defined it? Our fingers tangled as we both stroked the now smooth skin where a gaping wound had been hours ago.

Vamp saliva was amazing.

Moving as quietly as possible, I made my way to the bathroom and freshened up as best I could, considering the need for silence. I was feeling so much better. There was no pain anywhere, and I was clear-headed and felt strong. If it weren't for the apartment full of people, I would've been ready to go.

Zey was stretched out on his back on one side of the bed.

"I must rest now," he said telepathically. I frowned at him, increasingly irritated that I couldn't speak. He must've seen the questions in my eyes.

"It is similar to what you call sleep. A state of unconsciousness during which my body does important repair and my mind recharges. But we only require about two hours every few days."

Damn! I wished I could function on such little sleep. I nodded and waved him off to sleep land as I lowered myself onto the bed next to him. There was only one bed and no other furniture. I figured I may as well get all the rest I could while we were forced to wait.

I felt a bit awkward laying down next to him, but he was unmoving and seemed to already be asleep, so I forced myself to close my eyes.

I dozed, unable to go back to sleep fully. I was too aware of the music and laughter on the other side of the door, of the potential danger if someone decided to sneak off for a hookup or a sober vampire heard us in here.

I was on my side, watching Zey's profile and contemplating my life, when his voice spoke in my mind.

"Are you watching me sleep, Sky?" He opened his eyes and turned his head to give me a teasing smile.

I pressed my lips together, holding in a chuckle and a few choice words.

"Rude and creepy." He shook his head.

I pinched the bridge of my nose and extended my hand in a choking motion. I didn't know how else to express my irritation.

"How is your injury?" he asked, flipping onto his side to face me.

Unable to tell him that it was pretty much healed before he went to sleep—as he'd seen for himself—I moved the blanket and hiked my leg up so he could see. He reached out and prodded the spot with his warm, gentle fingers. The skin was perfectly smooth, like nothing had happened at all.

"*Remarkable*," he said, his gaze focused on where his hand still caressed my thigh.

I frowned and cocked my head. He was the one that wasn't remotely affected by bullets and could recover from seemingly anything as long as he was hydrated. Why did he think my healing was remarkable when his was so much better?

But obviously I couldn't ask him in that moment. Because of the whole needing-to-stay-silent thing, but also because I was distracted by the goosebumps that sprung up on my leg.

The room was warm and comfortable, and I couldn't even pretend that my skin was tingling because of anything other than his touch.

Zey cocked his head to the side, a curious expression on his face as he lifted his fingers off my thigh. Almost instantly, he returned his hand to my leg, running his palm over the raised bumps gently. His depthless eyes sparkled with wonder as he dragged his hand down my leg, lifting up on his elbow so he could reach all the way to my ankle.

The goosebumps rose in the wake of his touch, like every fiber of my being, down to my skin, was beckoned by his silent call.

Using just his middle finger, he drew a featherlight path down the outside of my foot, all the way to my pinkie toenail. Then he retraced his path.

His gaze and his touch followed all the way back up my leg to the spot where I'd been injured. But he didn't stop where he started. He kept going, caressing my skin higher and higher. He followed the curve of my hip and dipped his fingers under the band of my underwear like he needed to make sure no inch of skin was left untouched as he passed.

As his exploration reached the curve of my waist, I

jerked involuntarily. He'd accidentally found my ticklish spot. Hand hovering over my sensitive skin, he whipped his head up to look at me.

"*Did I hurt you?*" he asked, his eyes boring into me, as invasive as his words in my mind.

I shook my head and held his gaze. I'd have to explain tickling to him later.

Slowly, he returned his hand to my waist, watching me intently. I couldn't make myself look away, and he didn't seem to want me to.

My T-shirt had ridden up, and when he reached the fabric gathered at my ribs, he paused. It felt like sparks of soft electricity were flowing over my skin in waves, not letting the goosebumps settle down. My nipples were so hard, I felt like they might cut through the fabric of my T-shirt.

He stared at me—a question in his eyes even though he could've asked it mentally. It felt like we were on the precipice of something dangerous. But I wasn't thinking about consequences at that point. I just wanted him to keep touching me, keep making me *feel*.

I answered his wordless question by covering his hand with mine and guiding it up my ribs and under the shirt. His fingers caressed the curve of my breast, and my lips parted on a shaky exhale.

Lust was clear in his eyes, but the curiosity was strongly present too as he continued his exploration of my body. His fingers rubbed my taut nipple. He went back and forth, feeling the firm bud on his fingers, his palm, relentlessly teasing me with the gentle pressure without even meaning to.

Impatient, I arched my back, pushing my chest into his hand. Zey was nothing if not a fast learner, regardless of his intuitive learning mojo. He covered my breast with his big hand and kneaded, his thumb rubbing my nipple firmly.

Before he moved to my other breast, he shoved my T-shirt up so he could watch what he was doing. Then he repeated the slow tease on the other side, massaging gently before grabbing it.

I writhed under his touch. I'd never been this turned on from someone touching my tits before. We hadn't even kissed for fuck's sake! But then, no one had paid them such thorough attention before either.

Zey scooted down a bit and moved closer. His hard arousal pressed against my thigh, and my lust kicked up a notch at the proof of his body responding. He bent his head and licked the underside of one breast, then the other. My breathing was getting shallower with every moment.

While his curious hand kneaded one mound, his tongue explored the other on a sure path to my aching nipple. He wrapped his mouth around it and swirled his tongue around the tip.

A breathy moan escaped my lips as pleasure shot through my body and landed square between my thighs.

He lifted his head, a bit of saliva stretching between his full bottom lip and my nipple for half a second.

"You must be silent, Sky," he admonished as he pinned me with his stare. I bit my lip to keep from making more wanton sounds and from telling him to go fuck himself . . . or me. I bit so hard, I made it bleed.

With a frown, he reached up and gently tugged on my lower lip with his thumb until my teeth released it.

"Why are you hurting yourself?" He glared at my mouth.

Why are you asking questions when you know I can't answer them? I thought, darting forward to nip his thumb.

My teeth quickly gave way to my tongue, and I wrapped my lips around it as I sucked gently.

Zey's eyes hooded, and he shivered lightly. I released his thumb and grinned. Let's see how well he could stay silent when being tortured.

I rose up slowly and guided him onto his back. Straddling his hips, I removed my T-shirt.

I let my weight settle onto him fully. He was rock hard and the urge to roll my hips, get that friction where I needed it, was almost impossible to resist.

Zey's hands went to my hips, gripping firmly, fingers digging into the soft flesh there. His lips parted. He looked like he wasn't sure if he should hold me there or maneuver me so I'd start rocking.

His gaze locked with mine, and I leaned over him. My tits brushed his bare chest as I moved closer and closer to his face. Slowly, deliberately, I brushed the very tip of my tongue over his bottom lip.

A sharp knock on the door made us both freeze.

I held my breath, my full focus on the outside of the little room. It was quiet. There was no music, no raucous laughter.

"Sky?" Mitch called through the door. "Party's over. You can come out now."

I released the breath I was holding and sagged with relief. When had the party even ended? I was so wrapped up in Zey and his wandering hands that I'd completely let my guard down. Stupid!

"Coming!" I crawled off him and the bed, summoning myself some clothes and getting dressed quickly.

"That was the most stressful party of my entire existence," Mark groaned. Next to him, Mitch was slumped in his chair, looking like he was in full agreement.

"I feel like I'm hungover and also still drunk." Mitch dragged a hand down his face.

We were seated around their dining table, the mess of a massive party surrounding us. Zey had cleared half the table of bottles and trash while I cooked up a big pile of bacon and eggs. The least I could do after they saved my ass was use their food to cook myself (and them) a meal. Although Mitch looked like he was more likely to throw up, his plate untouched.

"We'll be out of your hair really soon," I said, scraping my plate, then gesturing to Mitch's. "You gonna eat that?"

He slid the plate towards me. Healing from a massive wound and infection really worked up a girl's appetite.

I wolfed it down quickly, acutely aware of the fact we were rapidly outstaying our welcome.

"OK, hand it over." I held my hand out. Zey pulled the Onuei out of his pants pocket. Mitch was a similar build and had given him some clothing he was planning to get rid of anyway. So now we sat at the table, accidentally wearing matching outfits. The black pants and sweater hugged his solid frame perfectly, and the boots completed the look.

He placed the hand crank in my palm.

"What the hell is that?" Mark sounded like he wasn't sure if we were crazy or he was.

"It's better if you don't know," I said before Zey could glare them both to death.

Healed, fed, and rested, it was much easier to focus on what my ability was showing me. The ribbons were definitely reaching towards Brazil, and I could now see a more specific area.

Opening my eyes, I sighed and handed the hand crank back to Zey.

"Hey, do you guys know any witches who could open a portal?" I asked, trying my best to sound casual and failing.

"You have got to be fucking kidding me," Mark huffed.

"Mark, I would not be sitting here nursing this hangover if it wasn't for Sky," Mitch reminded him without even lifting his head.

Unable to deny the love of his life, Mark huffed again, got to his feet, and pointed a finger at me. "Fine, but this makes us even."

"Absolutely." I nodded, and he left without another word.

"There's a witch a few floors down. She's high most of the time, so her magic can be unpredictable, but she's usually at her best in the mornings," Mitch explained, lifting his head.

"Thank you," I said, genuine gratitude in my voice and my eyes.

He reached across the table and took my hand. "Mark can be an asshole, but we both know that we'll never be even for what you did for us, Sky."

I squeezed his hand back while Zey watched us with a thoughtful look on his face.

Mark returned quickly with an elderly witch in tow. She was wearing faded polka-dot pajamas and a cardigan with a rip near the pocket, her gray hair all over the place.

"This better be worth my while, bloodsucker," the old witch croaked, glaring at everyone in the room.

"I'll make it worth your while," I said, getting to my feet.

"What do you want?" she grunted.

"A portal to Macapá, Brazil. How much?"

"You sure it's a good idea to portal into a House's territory when you're . . . in your current predicament?" Mark cautioned.

"We have no choice." I gave him a tight smile.

"Three cases of VitaBrew and a sachet of viloss dust." The witch made her demands and turned to leave. "Wake me up when you have my payment."

Viloss dust was made from drying and grinding up a flower that grew in the fae realm. It was a weed-like plant there, completely innocuous—but to all other species, it was a powerful hallucinogenic. It was outlawed in most House territories, but this was No Man's Land, and you could buy the stuff at the nearest market. Naturally, I had several sachets in my secret storage spot.

I summoned the three cases of VitaBrew one by one and set them on the dining table, followed by the palm-sized sachet of viloss dust. It was enough to get at least a dozen bear shifters off their faces—three times over.

"I have it right here," I said, stopping the witch halfway to the door. She turned with a slight frown, then zeroed in on the viloss dust and came back over with a bit more enthusiasm in her step.

Immediately, she held her hands out and started muttering the spell under her breath. She was breathing hard a few minutes later, but a glowing bowl of magic had appeared in her arms, swirling in rhythm with her words.

"The sacrifice," she said with a quick glance at me before refocusing on her spell.

I grabbed my fighting knife from its sheath and quickly sliced a deep cut in my forearm. Zey made a sound of alarm and went to reach for me, but I fixed him with a glare and held my bleeding arm over the magical bowl. I waited for the witch to nod that it was enough before removing it.

Mark surprised me by gripping my wrist and licking

the gash in my arm, his saliva healing the cut. Before I could thank him, the old witch clapped her hands together and a sound much louder than a regular clap reverberated through the apartment. All witches performed spells differently, but this was the first time I'd seen this particular technique. It was like she had collapsed the bowl of magic and my blood sacrifice in on itself. Her eyes glowed as she separated her hands, throwing her arms out wide.

A portal appeared before us, magic spinning intensely around a hole in the air that showed a quiet, cobbled street and what looked like a park at the end of it.

The old witch stepped around us, grabbing her payment and completely disinterested in what happened from here on out.

With a chorus of thank-yous and a promise to never show my face at their door again—unless I *wasn't* being hunted by every House on the planet—we stepped through the portal.

Being in any House's territory for any amount of time was not a good idea. Most members of Sea and Serpentine had some kind of affinity for water or were water-based supes (like mermaids), so their territory was pretty much all of the large bodies of water on the planet. But they also kept a small section of land where they had their House head-quarters and could deal with business on dry ground. Unfortunately, the Onuei was somewhere within this territory.

It was early afternoon in Macapá, and the strong sun was punishing. The portal disappeared quickly, and we ducked into the shade of a nearby building. The old witch seemed to have dumped us on the outskirts of town, thank-fully. It was quiet, and our arrival had gone unnoticed.

Zey pulled out the Onuei and handed it over before I could even ask for it. He wouldn't meet my gaze.

Had I insulted him somehow? Or did he feel weird? I wasn't sure if he felt awkward—if it was even something they had where he was from—but I was probably feeling awkward enough for the both of us.

I was no stranger to hookups, one-night stands, even the occasional relationship, but this morning after felt different somehow. Maybe it was because he was a totally different species, maybe because we still had to work closely together for the unforeseeable future. Maybe it was because I wanted to do it again, somewhere we weren't likely to get interrupted.

Whatever! I didn't have time for this.

I closed my eyes and let my power do what it did best. We were closer to the second Onuei now, and I had the first one to guide me in what I was looking for. The ribbons in my mind unfurled immediately, snapping in my mind's eye as they rushed towards their target. They were pulling me towards the busiest part of town—right on the edge of the water.

Zey took my free hand, his warm fingers wrapping around mine. I gasped and gripped onto him as a rush of power surged through me. A thinner, more fragile ribbon appeared, tugging me gently in the direction of the third Onuei. But I focused on the thick, strong one leading me to . . .

"Fuck," I breathed, opening my eyes.

"What's wrong?" Zey finally looked at me, concern clear in his gaze. His hand tightened around mine.

"I know exactly where the second Onuei is," I said. He started caressing the back of my hand gently with his thumb. I was done seeking; I didn't need to touch him to lock onto what I was trying to find anymore, but left my hand in his. It felt nice to have the connection after that weirdness.

Zey didn't badger me to tell him more or demand we get moving immediately like he usually did. He just stood there, looking at me, touching me, waiting patiently.

I didn't want to tell him what I was about to tell him. I didn't want to disappoint him. I had no idea why I gave a shit when barely twenty-four hours ago I'd been ready to fry his ass and leave him at the dump with all the other Vuulectians.

"I can clearly see where it is, down to the specific corner of a specific room, and I know exactly how to get there but . . ." I cringed. "I don't see how we're going to be able to get past the fence, let alone into the building."

"Where is it, Sky?" he asked, serious but missing the derisive scowl I'd come to expect from him whenever he was told something he didn't like.

"The Onuei is in the headquarters of the House of Sea and Serpentine."

CHAPTER 13

The Houses had a long-standing truce established after the Great Sacrifice. In theory—and to be fair, most of the time in practice too—they worked together to govern the world and the melting pot of supernatural species that the Earth now was. But anyone who thought the Houses didn't have friction was a fool.

The House of Spirit and Sapphire and the House of Sea and Serpentine weren't allies. But they weren't enemies either. Empress Asbesta, a water goddess and the leader of Sea and Serpentine, was vicious and ambitious. Her House was cutthroat—she was not an easy ally to make and not someone you'd want as an enemy.

Zey and I had made our way through the city as discreetly as possible, blending into crowds and avoiding any sign of House officials. I felt defeated, but Zey had talked me into getting a closer look at what we were dealing with.

We sat on a park bench, partially obscured by shrubbery, across the road from the impressive building where the House of Sea and Serpentine had their HQ. The property sat right on the water, the elaborate gardens stretching all the way to the edge. A high wrought iron fence encircled the entire compound.

"There are no guards," Zey said. "We could just walk in. Or maybe swim."

"None that you can see." I rested one elbow on the back of the bench and readjusted my cap so it was a little lower. "There are at least four sentries on the roof," I said, keeping my gaze down. "I can only spot two, but I guarantee there are more on the other side of the building. And the water may look calm but trust me, there are dozens of mermaids down there."

Zey glanced up and hummed.

"It is a place of business and governance, just like my House," I explained. "So yes, members of the public can come and go through the main entrance. But you bet your ass, those sentries are watching for threats, and in case you forgot, we're the biggest threats in the world at the moment."

I rolled my eyes and almost laughed when Zey did the same. Neither one of us was particularly impressed with how we were being portrayed.

"I've never been here, but there will definitely be guards inside."

"You will certainly be recognized," Zey conceded. "But I can take on the appearance of anyone and walk right by them."

"True, but that will only get you past those main gates, probably through the main doors at the end of that long-ass drive, maybe into some of the offices on the ground floor. The Onuei is in a room on the third floor on the other side of the building. I guarantee you, access to that area is restricted to members of Sea and Serpentine, most likely those with seniority."

"Then I will take the form of one of them," Zey stated like it was obvious.

I narrowed my gaze at him. "And what if the doors are spelled like they were in the building in Melbourne? You may be able to *look* like anyone, but magic knows if the energetic signature is wrong. What if there's some magical form of security, like a silent alert, or a combination, or even nonmagical systems that require a code or a key. What if someone speaks to you, thinking you're the person whose appearance you've taken? What if—"

"Alright," he cut me off, "you've made your point."

I folded my arms and dropped it, even though I still had at least a dozen scenarios that illustrated how this could go wrong.

"It's impossible." I shrugged, shaking my head.

"I admit, I was a little hasty in my impatience to get to the Onuei," Zey said, "but nothing is impossible, Sky. There is a way; I know it."

"How?" I huffed, getting frustrated. "Just because you want something to be true doesn't make it so. Shit doesn't work like that here, Zey."

"You can find a way," he stated matter-of-factly, like it was obvious I could figure this shit out.

"What makes you so . . . sure . . ." I trailed off as my gaze wandered down the street, where I knew the mouth of the Amazon River was. The portal to the world of angels and demons was deep in the rainforest. It was under constant watch by the Portal Guard, but not as much as the headquarters of Sea and Serpentine, and it was in No Man's Land.

"You've thought of something, haven't you?" Zey drew

my attention back to him. He was wearing a self-satisfied grin.

"Maybe," I huffed, reluctant to admit he was right, even as some semblance of a plan started to form in my mind.

"I knew you could do it." He brushed a stray bit of hair off my neck. The contact made me shiver.

I cleared my throat. "There might be a *possibility* of a *chance* that we could find a way in, but you're not going to like it."

"Why?"

"Because we have to get further away from the Onuei to find a way to get our hands on it."

"How far?" His eyes narrowed.

"A world away." I sighed, liking where this was going less and less as I questioned my own sanity for even considering it.

Zey followed my gaze. "You wish to go through a portal?"

"I don't know if *wish* is the right word but . . . there's someone on the other side that may be able to get us into the House headquarters."

"Great!" He slapped his knees and went to get up, ready to march right up to the portal and get us captured or killed. I threw an arm across his chest, stopping him.

"Easy, tiger. It's not that simple."

"Why are you referring to me as a large jungle cat?"

I completely ignored his question. "The person I'm thinking of, they're not a friend, not like Sabrina or even Mark and Mitch. They're just as likely to hand us over to the House of Sea and Serpentine as they are to help us. Not to mention we can't just waltz up to the portal and wander through it. There are guards and . . . ugh, can't anything ever be easy?" I grumbled.

"It is a risk. I understand." Zey turned his body towards mine and took both my hands in his. "But if you think this is our best option, then I am willing to take it if you are."

"Where's this sudden unwavering faith in me coming from?" I frowned. Zey dropped my hands and his gaze from mine.

"You have proven yourself—in ability and honor." He shrugged.

"Did . . . did you just give me a compliment?" I teased, my lips twitching with amusement.

"I have no idea what you're referring to," he sniffed. "I am simply stating facts."

"Uh-huh." Now it was me wearing the self-satisfied smile.

It was a shitty, dangerous plan, but it was the best and only one we had. I reminded myself I had nothing to lose. If there was ever a time to take a gamble, now was it.

"Alright, let's get this shit show on the road." I got to my feet and led the way down the street. Remaining vigilant, we made our way to the water where we "borrowed" someone's motorboat. Sea and Serpentine's territory on land barely covered the main Macapá area, but it extended quite far up the river. Unfortunately, it was the fastest way to reach the portal.

I felt the magic of the Sea and Serpentine border as we got close, but there were no visible signs of it. There was a slight pressure as we passed through, and I held my breath. I half expected a dozen mermaids to come shooting out of the murky water to apprehend us, but we zipped along without incident. Fortunately, like all other Houses, Sea and Serpentine was more concerned with who was entering their territory than who was leaving it.

It was dusk by the time we reached the dock, deep in a

remote part of the Amazon. There was a well-worn path through the rainforest to the portal, and we didn't waste any time heading up it. We were rapidly losing light, and I preferred to not be stuck in a remote rainforest with things that could eat me. So, despite the humid heat, we set a fast pace.

It was fully dark when we reached the portal. There were a few bars and restaurants and a small market that had sprung up in the area. The guardhouses and several other dwellings were spread a little further out in the trees—literally. They were treehouses. It was a pretty remote portal, so it was nowhere near as busy as some others. At this time of night, most businesses were closed, and not many people were around other than the ever-present Portal Guard. On the one hand, it was good because there were fewer people to potentially recognize us. On the other hand, there were fewer distractions for the Portal Guard to focus on.

"This area is No Man's Land, like all areas around a portal," I explained to Zey, leaning on a tree around a bend in the path. We were about twenty feet away from the gap in the massive netting that sat high up in the treetops, covering the entire area. The net was spelled with powerful magic and was there to help the Portal Guard do its job—an extra precaution at a portal that led to a world where everyone had wings. "No House has jurisdiction here. The guards' main job is to monitor the portal and make sure whatever comes through to Earth is not dangerous. They're not as uptight about people going the other way, but still . . . they could decide to capture and hand us in just as easily as they could let us pass."

"How do we convince them to do the latter? Can we pay them?"

"We could try, but in my experience, most portal guards

would take offense to that. They're all about honor and shit." I rolled my eyes. "I think if we wait until it's late and they're tired and bored, we might be able to surprise them and rush through. Once we're on the other side of the portal, they won't care either way."

"Perhaps there is an easier way," Zey mused, his gaze moving between the individual guards.

"Like what?"

"Do you trust me?"

"Nope," I answered immediately. He gave me an unamused look, tinged with a bit of irritation.

"Tough shit. Need I remind you we're working towards the same goal here?"

"Oh my god, did you just curse for the first time?" I covered my mouth with my hand, then pressed it to my chest. "Oh, they grow up so fast."

Zey ignored my sarcasm. Unfortunately, he was learning quickly that was the best way to deal with my snark. He just gave me a flat look as he shifted.

He shrank a little, and his hair turned blond. His features remained masculine, but he added some stubble, and his lips became thinner. Without a clue as to what he was planning, I watched him turn away and march towards the portal.

I couldn't have stopped him if I'd tried. The portal guards spotted him right away. They remained relaxed but alert. It wasn't unusual to have people approach a portal. Even as Zey got closer, two angels flew through the portal, landed to speak briefly with two guards, and stepped out through the gap in the netting just as Zey stepped in. I moved further into the shadows as the angels approached, but once they were out of the net, they just took flight anyway.

While all that was happening, Zey reached the nearest guard and started talking to him. They both laughed lightly, and Zey touched the man's arm. I frowned. Was he *flirting*?

I ground my teeth. What the hell was this supposed to achieve? Then I ground them a little harder when I realized I was jealous.

"*Sky.*" Zey's voice in my head startled me, and I focused. He was still chatting with the guard, having a grand old time. "*Come over now. Act frazzled, like you're running late.*"

I pulled a face and echoed his words in a snarky voice, but then I mussed my hair up, took a few fast breaths, and started jogging over. When Zey glanced over his shoulder, I waved at him and called, "Sorry!"

"There she is," Zey said to the guard, then leaned in close and whispered something in his ear. They both laughed as they watched me run up.

Planning my revenge in my head, I stopped in front of them and leaned my hands on my knees, making a show of breathing heavily.

"Sorry that took so long," I huffed, standing up straight.

"That's alright, gave me a chance to get to know Sven here." Zey winked at Sven. I threw up a little in my mouth but forced my smile to widen. "We'd better get going though."

"Right." I nodded. "Don't wanna be late for the . . . our . . . thing."

Talking over me a bit, Zey turned to Sven and said: "So, next Monday, right? Afternoon shift?"

"Yep. I'll be here." Sven was pretty much ignoring me completely; he was so focused on Zey. But a quick glance around told me one of the other guards was watching us closely, eyes narrowed. Like he was trying to figure out why I looked familiar, maybe.

"I'll see you then, Sven." Zey touched his shoulder one last time and took off for the portal. I fell into step next to him and, to my utter astonishment, we just . . . stepped through it and into the land of angels and demons.

CHAPTER 14

"What did you say to him?" I demanded as soon as we were on the other side of the portal.

"Nothing of importance." Zey shrugged, shifting his features back into his usual appearance. I took off up the path. Better keep moving in case one of those guards realized who we were and decided to report it.

"Those guys all have sticks up their butts—they don't just let people through portals so easily. Shit, I don't think I've ever even seen a portal guard smile! How did you do that?"

Zey turned wide eyes to me. "They have *sticks* up—"

I cut him off, "Expression indicating an uptight manner." Gods! Now I was sounding more like him.

"I changed my appearance to what he would find most appealing and employed some preliminary mating rituals. Where are we going?"

"Hah!" I spun to face him and poked him in the chest. "I knew you were flirting!"

Was it just me, or did that come out sounding accusatory?

Zey canted his head to the side and gave me an amused look. He grabbed my finger where it was jabbing into his chest but didn't remove it—he just kind of . . . held it there.

"Are you jealous?" he said, his face splitting into a grin.

"No," I scoffed and extracted my finger from his grip to keep walking.

Thankfully he decided to drop it, instead repeating, "Sky, where are we going?"

"To Lapsus Manor," I said, knowing perfectly well that meant nothing to him.

"How far is this Lapsus Manor?"

"Just on the other side of this hill." I pointed up the path that twisted through the barren landscape.

Celestia—or Soleil, as the demons called it—was an odd realm where physics didn't seem to apply. All the angels lived in Sky City—a shimmering, ethereal, gargantuan part of Celestia that floated above everything else. All the demons lived in the dark, mysterious Magma City below ground. The lifeless area in between, where the portal had opened and where we were walking now, was called Dead Man's Land. A few fallen angels and demons lived in this neutral zone for various reasons, but I only knew one.

We were going to meet with him now.

Zey kept looking around as we walked, half like he was wary of our surroundings and half like he was fascinated by it all.

The underside of Sky City, which was more the size of an entire continent, loomed high above us.

In the distance, we could just make out a giant hole in the ground next to some rocky hills. The crater led to Magma City below ground, where the demons made their home. Nothing grew in Dead Man's Land between the two.

Wasteland was an understatement when it came to what the landscape looked like.

Thankfully, we didn't have to walk for days on end, and a brisk half-hour walk had us approaching our destination. Lapsus Manor was located right on the edge of the crater leading to Magma City. It wasn't long before the structure became visible, nestled into the side of the jagged, rocky hill.

"Lapsus Manor?" Zey asked as we approached.

"Lapsus Manor." I nodded. It was not the bricks-and-mortar kind of building that was common on Earth, nor was it anything like the glittering, awe-inspiring behemoth in the sky. I had no idea what Magma City below looked like, but I had a feeling it didn't resemble that either.

Lapsus Manor was the same beige, flat color as the wasteland beyond it. It would've completely blended into the landscape if it wasn't for the many windows reflecting the sun and the imposing glass doors in the center. They were at least three stories high, and I had no idea how anyone managed to move them. They must've weighed a ton.

I'd only been to this realm once, on House business, and I'd had to go to Lapsus Manor then too. It was only half a day's trip, consisting of a meeting and a lavish lunch, but Abraxos had still managed to get me alone and try to convince me to find something for him.

He rarely visited Earth, but every time he did, he tracked me down and tried to get me to find what he was after—sometimes with gifts and flirting, sometimes with threats and intimidation.

"So, what's the plan?" Zey asked as we approached the doors.

"Oh, now you want to talk plans? You seemed perfectly

148

happy to just do whatever you wanted back at the portal. Maybe I'll do the same. Maybe I'll flirt my way in."

"You're always welcome at Lapsus Manor, Sky Serpell," a deep voice said behind me. I turned just in time to see Abraxos land, his magnificent wings elegantly lowering him to the ground, the iridescent feathers shimmering even in the absence of sunlight. "But I'd be more than happy to flirt with you if you'd like."

"That won't be necessary," Zey said, coming to stand shoulder to shoulder with me.

Abraxos barely spared him a disinterested glance.

"Thanks, but I didn't come all this way to flirt." I gave him a thin smile.

"Then to what do I owe this great pleasure?"

I bristled, shifting my weight. This was going to suck. "I need your help."

Abraxos's smile widened, more a showing of teeth than an expression of amusement. "And why should I risk helping two dangerous fugitives wanted by half of Earth's Houses?"

"You heard about that, huh?"

"I make sure to stay abreast of relevant news from many realms," he said. His eyes were practically shining with greed, but he waited for me to say it.

"I'll find what you're looking for," I sighed. "If you help us get what we're looking for."

Abraxos took a deep breath and stared at Sky City above with something unfathomable in his gaze.

"Looks like we have a deal to make." He waved his arm towards his castle in a grand invitation. With a heavy heart, I followed him in, Zey keeping close to me.

We were shown in through the massive doors, past the grand entrance, and into a sitting room. Abraxos's manor seemed to be purposefully, defiantly drawing from its very surroundings in Dead Man's Land. There was a lot of stone—from marble floors, to ornately carved stone window and doorframes, to heavy, solid furniture that looked like it was carved out of the very ground they sat on.

Abraxos lowered himself into a throne-like chair with opulent cushions and a back that accommodated his wings. Zey and I sat on a backless bench across from him.

Several servants came in, setting fruit and pastries, teas and wine on the low table between us.

"Sky the Seeker," Abraxos purred as he poured himself a glass of wine. "What is it you seek?"

"What we seek is of no importance," Zey answered before I could. "The location is the obstacle."

Abraxos's smile hardened as he turned his gaze on Zey. "Is your name also Sky?"

I resisted the urge to shift a little closer, feeling weirdly protective. Last time I was here, I was safe by virtue of being a representative of the House of Spirit and Sapphire. This time, no one even knew I was here. Abraxos was a dangerous man.

"His name is Zey, and if you want to make this deal, you'll treat my companion with a modicum of respect," I said, sitting straighter and holding Abraxos's gaze. I was intimidated and my fingers itched to reach for my fighting knife, but I kept still. The only way to deal with people like this was to not back down.

After a painfully long, tense moment, Abraxos sighed and rolled his eyes as he sipped his wine. "Very well. *Zey*, tell me what it is you want from me."

"The item we're trying to procure is in the House of Sea and Serpentine's HQ. Sky seems to think you can get us safely and discreetly inside." Did I detect a hint of derision in Zey's voice?

I suddenly felt like a schoolteacher, making two boys shake hands and call a truce on their schoolyard tiff.

"So, you expect me to harbor two dangerous fugitives, lie to my House, and help you steal something from them?" Abraxos raised his brows, putting on an incredulous expression.

I narrowed my eyes. We both knew very well he had no interest in House politics on Earth and only remained a member because it was convenient for him at times. He had no qualms about any of this.

"The item does not belong to anyone of your House," Zey said. "It's hardly stealing. And the rest seems trivial to get what you really want."

Abraxos watched Zey thoughtfully as he leaned forward, his arm brushing mine, and popped a small, fluffy pastry into his mouth. Then his attention turned back to me.

"And in exchange, you'll summon the Orb of Sinne for me?" Now we were getting somewhere.

"I can't summon something I haven't touched before—not something that unique. There are limits to my magic, like all magic. But I can seek it and tell you where you can find it."

"Now." Abraxos leaned forward too, setting his wine down on the stone table with a clink. "Once I have the Orb of Sinne in my possession, I'll escort you to the House."

"No." I shook my head. "Once we safely and secretly reach the item we're looking for, I'll tell you where to find yours."

Abraxos clenched his teeth, clearly hating he wasn't getting everything he wanted immediately. "You will seek it now and tell me something so I can be sure you have indeed located it."

I nodded. "I can work with that."

"Then we have a deal." Abraxos grinned and held his hand out for me to shake. Before I could say anything, Zey piped in again.

"Just to clarify—you will do this as soon as possible, you will ensure we are safe and hidden, and you will get us to the item. Sky won't be telling you anything until what we're after is in our possession. Additionally, you will not make any plans to go back on your word once you have the information you want. No plotting to have us captured right after, no secret deals to undermine us, no—"

"Yes, yes," Abraxos cut him off impatiently. "No shady shit, as you humans like to say. Although you're not exactly human, are you, Zey?"

They stared each other down, and I felt like a schoolteacher again.

"Right. Anyway. Do we have a deal?" I held my hand out first this time, breaking their weird staring contest. Abraxos gave me his full attention and shook my hand firmly with a grin.

In the back of my mind, I imagined the sound of a prison cell door clanging shut. There was no going back now. We were locked into this shitstorm with a fallen angel I couldn't entirely trust. I wasn't sure what the Orb of Sinne was or what it did, but anything that was coveted so fiercely, and hidden so well, must be very powerful. I mean, look at the lengths we were going to in order to find the Onuei.

What other choice did I have?

Once I explained to Abraxos how my ability worked— that I needed something or someone with a connection to the item—he abandoned his wine halfway through the glass and marched us through his cavernous mansion.

There were people around, guards and servants, only a few angels and plenty of humans, but they were scarce. For the most part, the place felt eerily empty.

Partway up a staircase, he stopped us in front of a painting that was twice as tall as me and three times as wide. It was a battle scene with majestic angels and demons clashing on the ground and in the sky. When I didn't look at it directly, it seemed to move out of the corner of my eye, like the scene was coming to life for a brief moment. But that wasn't the interesting thing about it.

Abraxos flapped his wings and lifted himself into the air so he could point at something in the top right corner of the image.

"This is what it looks like." He gestured to an orb held in the arms of an angel flying away from the battle scene. It was about the size of a large decorative paperweight and appeared to glow from within. "The depiction is accurate, right down to scale."

I climbed a few more stairs and craned my neck for a better look, but it was so high up.

Abraxos landed on the step below me with a flourish.

"Allow me," he said, holding his arm out.

I glanced over his shoulder at Zey. He stood with his arms crossed, focused intently on the painting, a muscle in his jaw twitching.

Eager to get this over with as quickly as possible, I took Abraxos's hand. He pulled me in close and lifted me into his arms before flying me up to the corner of the painting. Nose-to-nose with the Orb of Sinne, I studied it, then took a picture on my phone.

Zey was silent as Abraxos returned me to my feet, and

we continued deeper into the house. In what appeared to be a study—walls lined with books, a big desk in the middle—he went to a cupboard and extracted a box.

It was wood, polished to a high shine and every corner smoothed out so there were no sharp edges to be seen. Inside was nothing but silk lining and a cushiony, soft place for the Orb of Sinne to sit.

"It used to be stored in this some three or four hundred years ago," Abraxos explained. "Do you have enough to seek?"

I didn't even want to know how he had come to have that in his possession.

"Let's find out." I sighed and stepped forward. With one more glance at the image on my phone, I reached out and placed my hand in the box. Closing my eyes, I focused on the energy of the item I was seeking. The Orb of Sinne must've been kept in the box for a very long time before they were separated. Its energetic signature was so strong, it almost felt like it was vibrating over my skin.

The ribbons responded immediately, snapping out in the direction of the Orb of Sinne almost violently. I gasped with the intensity of it and gripped the edge of the table with my free hand.

"Sky!" Zey's voice sounded distant, like I was underwater, and I was vaguely aware of tense voices and the flap of wings behind me. But I kept my focus on the ribbons and where they were taking me.

When the Orb of Sinne came into focus, it was so clear I almost felt like I could summon it. I wasn't even remotely interested in trying that though. Beside the fact that I didn't want to make it any easier for Abraxos to get his hands on this thing, I had a feeling straining so much would make me pass out—maybe even kill me. If I could do it at all.

Still . . . my power had grown in ways I couldn't have predicted since Zey and I had started searching for the Onuei. Maybe I really could summon something without having touched it. Now was as good a time to try as any. My connection to this particular item was so strong. It was practically *begging* me to summon it into my hands. I could almost feel the weight of it . . .

With a sharp inhale, I wrenched my hand off the box and forced my eyes open. Sweat was dampening my brow, and my breathing was labored.

I met Zey's worried gaze first, his familiar black eyes grounding me. Then I turned to Abraxos.

"Well?" He stepped forward, looking like he was fighting the urge to bounce on his toes in anticipation.

"I think it nearly killed me." I swallowed and cleared my dry throat. "But I found it."

CHAPTER 15

Whatever I was lying on was so soft that I wouldn't have been surprised if I found myself cuddled up on a cloud. I squinted one eye open to make sure I was, in fact, on a bed in Abraxos's mansion, then snuggled into the luxurious bedding a little more.

I hadn't slept this well in weeks, probably years. I guessed being manipulated by a magical object to try to push my power past its breaking point really took it out of a girl. And after our discussion last night, I knew there was no rush to get up. No one was chasing us; we weren't in a rush to get somewhere or run away from someone for the first time since Zey dragged me into his drama. So I indulged and let myself keep snoozing.

After I tracked down the Orb of Sinne, Abraxos tried to sneakily get more information out of me than what we agreed to. But even with a building headache and weak as I was, I didn't give it all away. Instead, I gave him a detail about how the Orb was protected, and he grudgingly agreed that it was confirmation I wasn't lying.

Then Zey insisted I sit down—probably because I was beginning to sway on my feet—and Abraxos had dinner brought into his study. I was absolutely starving, and I stuffed my face while we talked. Zey kept an arm around me the entire time. I didn't have the energy to tell him to back off and give me space . . . but also, it was kind of nice to be comforted when I felt so weak and vulnerable. Despite myself, I trusted the bastard.

The thought of food made me acutely aware of my stomach, which was empty and demanding to be filled, and my bladder, which was full and demanding to be emptied. Rolling onto my back, I stretched and opened my eyes. Judging by the amount of light spilling into the room, I'd slept for a long time—well into the day.

When we were shown to our room the night before, I'd beelined for the bed and was asleep before my body even completed the flop onto the pillow. So I took a moment to check out our accommodations for the next few days.

The room was lavish, like the rest of the manor. It was spacious, ostentatious, and airy. There was marble everywhere, artwork on the walls, gold detailing on the furniture, and luxurious bedding and cushions made from the finest fabrics.

Some of that ridiculously soft fabric slid down my body as I sat up, and I realized I wasn't fully clothed like I had been when I passed out. Someone had removed my shoes and clothes and left me in my underwear and tank top.

No prizes for guessing who that someone might be. It was thoughtful of him.

I frowned and scanned the room again. Abraxos had tried to put us in separate rooms, but Zey had insisted we remain together. But there was no sign of him anywhere.

"Zey?" I called, then cleared my throat. My voice was rough and croaky.

Just as I thought I'd have to delay breakfast to look for him—to make sure Abraxos hadn't murdered him for shits and giggles—he came rushing into the room. One entire wall was open, light, sheer curtains fluttering in the wind and revealing a terrace beyond. Zey smacked the delicate fabric out of the way and crossed the room in record time.

I leaned back so I wouldn't headbutt his midsection.

"Sky. You're awake. Good." He smiled and managed to look worried and relieved at the same time. "You have been asleep for eleven hours, thirty-eight minutes. I was worried something was not right, but you were breathing, and your body didn't appear to be in distress. Why are you sitting? Do you need help getting up? Can you feel your legs?"

I blinked up at him, then snorted and let out a deep laugh. He chuckled uncertainly while scanning my body for paralysis or something.

"Chill dude." I threw the covers back and got up. "See, legs work just fine. I just needed to sleep to recover from . . ." I waved my hand in the air. "Everything. Now I need to eat."

"There is a very large amount of food on the table outside." He took my hand and started to drag me that way, but I gently extracted it.

"Bathroom first." I patted him on the shoulder and headed in the direction of the only door other than the one to the room. With my hand on the handle, I paused and looked over my shoulder. "Thanks for last night, for making sure I was comfortable and whatever."

Zey gave me a gentle smile and a nod, and I escaped into the bathroom before he could say anything. I didn't often feel awkward around people. Even shifters didn't

scare me—much. But Zey had been acting more and more
. . . attentive or something. Caring? I wasn't sure it was all
about ensuring I lived long enough to lead him to his Onuei.

He'd definitely been jealous when Abraxos had flirted
with me. I didn't know what to do with this crap. He was
getting his things and going back to where he came from.
This was a business transaction.

Ugh! Who was I kidding? I'd been checking him out
since he chose his human form. Maybe the feeling was
mutual. Maybe . . .

I shook my head and used the bathroom as quickly as
possible. Like the rest of the mansion, the bathroom was all
marble walls and solid rock with ornate faucets. Not an
amenity was spared, and I took full advantage of the tooth-
brushes, soaps, razors, oils, and myriad other things in there.
I contemplated running a bath—in the tub carved out of
what looked like a massive amethyst—but decided it could
wait.

Wrapped in a fluffy robe, I made my way to the terrace,
my stomach constantly grumbling.

Zey stood at the railing, looking out over the landscape
and Sky City floating in the heavens. I plonked myself
down at the table laden with food and dug into the first
thing my fingers wrapped themselves around. Some kind of
fruit that tasted a bit like banana.

The terrace was as grand and opulent as our room,
with a table setting and two loungers. There was even a
pool tucked into one corner, although it looked more like a
naturally occurring grotto embedded in the cliff. There
was water trickling from a hole in the stone wall and
cascading over the edge of the terrace where the pool
ended.

I broke the silence as I poured myself some coffee. "Still

salty that we can't go racing into Sea and Serpentine HQ immediately?"

"Salty?" Zey turned to face me, his lips pulling up in an amused smile.

"You know—like, pissed."

He glanced down his front. "Are you insinuating I've soiled myself?"

I chuckled and shook my head as I picked a pastry covered in powdered sugar and leaned back in my chair. "No, it means annoyed, irritated. You know, despite the fact you've ruined my life, I'm gonna miss this."

"No. I have accepted this is the best course of action. I trust your judgement, Sky."

We'd discussed how Abraxos would deliver on his end of the deal over dinner the previous night. My head was pounding, but I was well enough to have the conversation. He pointed out that the easiest way to sneak us in would be when there were distractions. We all agreed on this. When he told us the best opportunity would be in a couple of days when the House of Sea and Serpentine would be hosting their yearly ball, Zey got a bit impatient. I was used to his incessant drive to get the Onuei and get them *now*, but Abraxos got rather defensive, and it nearly escalated into a fight. I pointed out that we already had one of the Onuei and the Lineg Legion didn't have any. Plus we only had one shot at this, and I wasn't interested in getting captured. Again.

This seemed to defuse the situation somewhat, and we headed to bed not long after, Zey still grumbling about having to wait and not trusting Abraxos. I guessed he'd slept on it and come to his senses.

"You are right about the Onuei." He pulled the hand crank out of his pocket and set it on the table. "Even if the

Lineg get the other two Onuei, they can't do anything without having all three. And they don't have you to search for them."

"That's right." I flashed him a smug smile. "I'm fucking awesome, and don't you forget it."

Popping the last of the pastry into my mouth, I got up and went to the railing, curious about what was beyond.

"Yes, you are," Zey said, and I could feel his gaze on me, but I was too focused on the terrifying drop below us to pay much attention.

Abraxos had built his home at the very precipice of a crater that led to Magma City. The water trickling out of our little pool looked like tiny droplets as it fell into the fathomless depths, swallowed up by the darkness before it ever reached the bottom.

"Damn, that's high as fu-uuu . . ." I trailed off and had to clear my throat when I returned my attention to our terrace.

Zey was no longer next to me. He'd made his way over to the grotto—but not before removing all his clothing. I stared with my coffee halfway to my mouth as he slowly waded into the water. His powerful thighs and perfect ass flexed with each leisurely step. I couldn't seem to tear my gaze away from the spot where the water slowly moved up his body, hiding more and more of him from view as he waded deeper. It wasn't until the water was up to his waist and he dipped his whole body under the surface that I shook myself out of it.

I took another sip of my coffee and started to make my way back inside, but I couldn't stop myself from glancing over again.

He was floating on his back, eyes closed and a serene look on his face, his junk just sitting there, resting on his stomach. The water looked very inviting, and it wasn't like I had anything else to do . . .

But I didn't have a bathing suit. *But neither does he!* I thought, reminding myself that I refused to be embarrassed by someone else's nudity—or be chased away from food by it!

Not that I was really interested in the spread on the table anymore.

I set my mug on the table and turned to the pool. I wore nothing under my robe, and I let it fall to the floor without hunching my shoulders or trying to hide my bits.

Zey opened his eyes and sat up as I stepped into the water. He watched the waterline as it moved up my body, just like I'd done to him moments earlier. A lot of shit had been confusing and uncertain lately, but there was no mistaking the heated look in his gaze.

The water was the perfect temperature and somehow felt softer than regular water. I sighed as I dipped my body in to my neck and propelled myself to the edge where it was trickling off the balcony.

"Abraxos may be a pain in the ass, and I may very well have started something chaotic for the angels and demons by giving him what he wants," I sighed, making a mental note to try to negate the damage when this was all over, "but you gotta hand it to the guy—he knows how to make his guests comfortable."

The water rippled gently over my skin as Zey made his way over and settled next to me with his back to the edge and his elbows resting on it.

"I fear we are more prisoners than guests," he said.

"Really?"

"There have been at least four guards outside our door

since we were shown to the room. I tried to leave to get you food while you slept, but they wouldn't allow it."

Ignoring the fact that he seemed to have made a habit of finding me food while I slept, I frowned, slightly worried. "What did they say?"

"That anything we required would be brought to us immediately, but they were under strict instructions to make sure we stayed in the room—for our protection, of course."

I was a little proud of how dry and sarcastic he sounded —he got that from me.

"Of course." I rolled my eyes. "Abraxos is protecting his interests, making sure what he wants most doesn't slip out of his grasp. But he won't wait any longer than absolutely necessary to fulfill his end of the bargain. We might technically be prisoners, but I think we're safe here."

"For now." Zey nodded.

"Yeah, there's no telling what he'll do once he has the location of the Orb, but we have three whole days to make our own plans."

Zey hummed and frowned slightly at the water, lost in thought. I felt kind of bad for ruining his water-induced bliss, so I decided to change the topic.

"Why did you choose this form?" I asked, folding my arms and resting them on the edge of the pool.

"The musculature and composition are well-suited to running and fighting—it is a warrior's body. The features are appealing to you, ensuring you'll be more amenable to providing assistance. And when you made me consider it that day in the hotel, the sum of its parts felt like me. The longer I remain in it, the more that feeling resonates."

"Hold up." I chuckled. He was always burying the lead.

"I'm glad that you're not walking around in a meat-suit that doesn't fit, but can we go back to the 'appealing to me' bit?"

"Are you mad? This is seen as manipulative by humans, right? That's not really something we have in Vuulectus."

"You don't have manipulation in—never mind." I waved that fascinating info off. "Had you told me this then, I probably would've been mad, but I dunno . . ." I shrugged. "I guess I know you better now, and I know it's just your nature—that you weren't doing it to hurt me or whatever."

"I would never hurt you, Sky." He fixed me with that intense, depthless look.

I glanced away, uncomfortable at his fervent declaration.

"How can you be so sure this form is appealing to me?" I smirked and turned my nose up slightly.

"Intuitive learning." One side of his mouth quirked into a little smile.

"Well maybe it's glitching or something. How can you be sure I don't prefer a female form?"

He cocked his head to the side thoughtfully, but with an amused, teasing edge to the expression. Slowly, his features shifted, his shoulders narrowed, his chest expanded into breasts. Within moments, a female version of Zey sat in the water next to me. It was still him—her. The key features that I'd come to know so well were still there. Her hair was the same dark brown, but longer, the ends floating on the surface of the water. The facial features were very similar, but softer and without that sharp masculine jawline. The eyes . . . the eyes were the same. That depthless black with the slightest hint of my own amber drawing me in like a moth to a flame.

"Hmmm." A thoughtful look crossed her stunning face.

"Perhaps I did make an error. You seem to be rather taken by this form."

Even her voice was softer, gentler somehow.

"Do I?" My voice had gone breathy. I'd admitted to myself that I was attracted to Zey, but I hadn't expected to be just as taken by the female version.

She dropped one of her elbows from the edge and turned to face me. The water hovered around her nipples, drawing my eyes to the swell of her breasts. They were a little bigger than mine, and I had an urge to see if they felt the same in my hands.

"You do," Zey said, moving in closer, brushing my wet hair over my shoulder. I turned so we were facing each other. Inch by inch, we leaned closer, our eyes greedily exploring every inch of skin visible above the water.

I moaned softly when our lips connected, my hand moving through the water to her waist. I hadn't been expecting just how soft the kiss would be. It still felt like kissing Zey, and when I closed my eyes, it was like I could sense the very essence of him in every spot where we touched. But on a very physical level it was . . . different. Not better or worse, just different.

I'd never been with a woman before, never found myself interested. I might have to reassess that.

Zey ran gentle fingers up my arm and wrapped her own around my neck. My hand at her waist went to her back. As we drew each other closer, our breasts squished together. I gasped and pulled back, glancing down, mesmerized by the water lapping at the soft mounds, at the way they rose and fell with our synched-up breathing.

She tilted my face back up to hers and kissed me hard. Our tongues battled for dominance as our hands explored. Her tits were as soft as mine, I quickly found out, but they were much more fun to play with. Her ass was juicy, her curves made even more tantalizing by the water all around us.

Fingers much smaller than what I was used to slid between my legs and stroked me. We both moaned, panting into each other's mouths, our kisses turning messy. The very tip of one delicate finger teased at my entrance, but then it was gone.

Zey pressed her forehead to mine, her hands gripping my waist.

"Sky," she panted, my name a plea and a reproach on her lips. "I know you're enjoying this form, and I promise we can explore this more some other time, but I crave carnal pleasure with you in my male form. I need to be inside you."

"Yes." I nodded without hesitation. "Fuck me, Zey."

I ignored the little voice in my head pointing out that there probably wouldn't be another time to explore this. If this was all the time we had together, I refused to spend it worrying about shit I couldn't control.

Zey shifted faster than I'd ever seen him do it before. The hands on my waist grew rougher, bigger, the grip firmer as he loomed over me in the full glory of his perfectly male chosen form.

"Say it again," he demanded, those eyes boring into mine, one hand coming up to grip my chin.

I had to fight not to whimper the words, to have them come out as strongly as I felt them.

"Fuck me, Zey," I said with certainty, meeting his gaze.

He growled and yanked me against his strong chest, his mouth devouring mine. The kiss was intense like before, but less gentle, more familiar.

I couldn't hold the whimper back as I wrapped my arms around his neck and surrendered to this feeling.

Gripping my thighs, he lifted me and turned in the water to press my back against the wall of the pool.

The sun glinted off the water and made Zey look like he was glowing. His wet, golden skin glistened, his hair shined, every part of him looked like it was glowing in the sun. Everything other than those eyes. The blackest black remained flat and unfathomably deep.

His lips crashed to mine once more, the water splashing around us as we clawed at each other. Our hands explored with more urgency now, less caress and more fingers digging into flesh, teeth scraping, legs tightening to bring him closer.

He broke the kiss to lick up my jaw, sucking at the sensitive spot below my ear. I reached between us and stroked him in the water. I groaned when I felt how hard he was, how ready to fill me. My core clenched at the idea of it, and my hips rocked forward of their own volition.

"I know you haven't done this before," I panted as he continued to kiss and lick my neck, his hands exploring, "at least, not in this form. I don't even know if sex is the same where you're from. Do you guys even *have* sex? Never mind, doesn't matter. Point is, I can talk you through it, although you seem to be doing OK so far."

He lifted his head to look at me. "Sky, you're babbling."

"I know, I just—" I gasped, my words dying in my throat as he pushed two fingers inside me without preamble. He barely teased me with a few pumps before removing them to rub circles against my clit.

I moaned and clung to his shoulders, but his fingers left just as abruptly as before.

"Zey, you need to keep—" he cut me off with his mouth to mine. After a brief searing kiss, he pulled away again.

"Shhhh," he hushed, his mouth so close to mine that I could feel the air brush my lips. *Did this asshole just shush me? When I was trying to teach him how to fuck?* The audacity.

Before I could get any more outraged, he gripped me firmly by the ass, adjusted the angle of my hips, and slid his cock inside me. I groaned softly, throwing my head back as he filled me slowly. Inch by blissful inch, Zey slid into me until he was balls deep, our hips flush.

For a split second, I worried about protection, but I'd paid a hefty price for a potion that prevented pregnancy and infection for up to three years. And I wasn't even sure his species could get me pregnant.

My breathing was labored, and my internal walls clenched around his hardness involuntarily. I wanted him to start moving, thrusting, but I equally wanted him to just stay right where he was. I was so acutely aware of every inch of him, the delicious stretch of him. I wished I could remain suspended in that moment, on the very edge of something that promised to be explosive.

"I think I've got the hang of it," he said, his tone teasing.

I opened my eyes to find him smirking at me with a self-satisfied look on his face.

Instead of teasing him or throwing back a witty retort, I rocked my hips. I pulled back just enough to slide off his length a few inches, then ground forward to take him all the way in again.

The smug look was wiped off his face immediately, replaced by open-mouthed pleasure as his body stiffened and his hands dug into my ass.

I gave him a smirk back. He may have figured sex out—whether it was through his intuitive learning thing or just pure instinct—I had to give him that much. But I had years of experience on him, and I was going to blow his goddamn mind before we crawled out of this pool.

Both of us were determined to make the other feel amazing with our sexual prowess. It didn't take us long to find a good rhythm. With one hand on the edge of the pool for balance, Zey pounded into me. I dug my heels into his ass and rocked my hips, meeting his thrusts. Water splashed around us tumultuously as we moaned and panted and fucked the absolute shit out of each other.

I felt my orgasm building swiftly, my whole body starting to feel tingly.

"I'm gonna . . . holy shit, Zey, I'm gonna . . ."

He watched my face with fascination and something like greed as his thrusts became more frantic. In the next second, he gritted his teeth and threw his head back as he came hard. The muscles in his neck stretched taut as he groaned his release.

I was so damn close. If he'd kept pumping into me for just another few seconds, I would've shattered right with him, but the rhythm was interrupted, and my orgasm evaded me.

The groan I released was more frustration than anything, and Zey snapped his head down to look at me. His eyes roamed over my still-writhing body, and a look of determination entered those eyes I loved.

Before I could tell him what I needed, he pulled out of me and gripped my waist. The muscles in his arms and shoulders flexed as he lifted me onto the edge of the pool. The back of my head and shoulders hit the glass railing as he dipped lower into the water.

He lifted one of my knees to rest over his shoulder and pushed the other out to the side as far as it would go, then lowered his mouth to my aching pussy.

I gripped his hair, and a guttural sound of pleasure and need left my throat at the feeling of his lips on me. I writhed under him, my hips rolling against him as he licked and sucked firmly—just how I needed it.

I was so close already, and my body was responding easily to how thoroughly he was devouring me. My runaway orgasm was speeding right back, promising to be even more intense.

His fingers dug into my thigh, keeping me open wide to him. His other hand came up under his chin, and he pushed two fingers inside.

"Fuck!" I yelled, my release *right. Fucking. There.*

At my outburst, he looked up. Forcing my eyes to stay open and locked with his, I shook through my orgasm, coming all over his face.

Instead of stopping and saying something cocky or teasing, Zey just kept going. His mouth and fingers kept the same rhythm even as I tugged on his hair and tried to wriggle away. Within seconds, he wrung another orgasm out of me, making my vision go blurry at the edges.

He pulled back softly, but I couldn't see if he was wearing that cocky smile, nor did I care. My limbs were jelly, and I started to slide into the water as he released me. I made a half-assed attempt to stop my body from flopping into the pool like a seal, but gave up.

Zey caught me in his arms, and I didn't even care that he chuckled as he lowered me into the water. It felt like bliss on my over sensitive skin. He walked me around the pool for a few moments, and I let my limbs drag through the water, relaxing fully.

Letting my legs drop, he then floated us back over to the edge. He turned me gently, and I leaned on the stone ledge where the water cascaded out of the pool. It trickled past, grazing my sides and arms as I relaxed my head on my forearms and let my legs dangle.

Zey stayed close, his hands caressing my back. I hummed and closed my eyes, thinking we were going to relax for a while, but no.

I guessed Vuulectians recovered faster than human men, even in their human forms, because Zey was hard as a rock and ready to slide into my sensitive pussy again already.

I wasn't complaining.

CHAPTER 16

As it turned out, we did actually have another opportunity to explore sex with Zey in his female form. With nothing much else to do for three days, we spent an obscene amount of time fucking. We did it on every surface of that room; we did it with Zey shifting into various celebrities; we did it with him in his original form, the area between his legs shifted into something ridged and curved and perfectly formed to hit all my favorite spots. He was able to shift only particular parts of his body if he chose, so sometimes he adjusted the size of specific appendages in the middle of sex. Every time I ate a meal, he would drop to his knees, push my legs apart, and eat one too.

Zey was ready to try just about anything; curious and open-minded in a way that only someone who'd grown up without Earth-specific social conditioning had.

It was the best sex of my life.

It was also the best sleep of my life. Between the constant state of post-orgasmic bliss, the amazing food, and the ridiculously comfortable bed, how could it not be?

In the moments between, we talked. We were both curious about the other's home realm, what it was like to live there, how it all functioned, why there were issues, and how we thought they could be fixed. Inevitably, those chats would turn more personal.

He asked about my parents, and I told him about my mother and how I'd never known my father but suspected he was a warlock—how else would you explain my powers and his complete absence? He asked about my experiences in the House of Spirit and Sapphire, about my friends, my relationships. He posed questions about my favorite food with the same calm curiosity as he prodded me about my sexual history and preferences. To him, it was all a matter of learning about the new species and world he'd been introduced to. He didn't understand that people might find some of his questions rude. I found them refreshingly honest.

For every question one of us had, it sparked another three for the other.

He told me more about being an advisor to the last True Leader of Vuulectus, how it had allowed him to see more of his world than most Vuulectians ever did. I asked about his parents and childhood too, and while he knew who his biological parents were, it seemed that "it takes a village to raise a child" was something that was taken quite literally in Vuulectus.

We talked about everything—from theories about systems of governance to random childhood memories.

There were a few moments where I actually forgot . . . everything. Who we were, why we were there in the first place, what was waiting for us back on Earth. But then I'd catch Zey with that pensive, uneasy look on his face, or I'd start thinking about what was happening back home while we were gone, and it would all come flooding back.

On the morning of the ball, I was startled awake by a knock on our door. Zey was already opening it by the time I shot up in bed and summoned my knife from across the room. He spoke softly with whomever was in the hallway for a brief moment and closed the door again.

"Abraxos has issued orders for everyone to be ready to go through the portal in a few hours. They're sending up food and servants to prepare us, whatever that means." He frowned at the floor as he spoke.

When I didn't respond, he looked up. He looked as dejected and conflicted as I felt. The bubble was bursting. Our time together was coming to an end, and something inside me was breaking at the sense of cold hard reality invading our happiness. I realized I'd made a colossal mistake letting my guard down with Zey. I was a fool to think I could just have some casual fun with him. I'd already been starting to feel more for the complicated creature before we'd even got here, and now . . . yeah, I was screwed.

My distress was surely written all over my face—I'd stopped hiding from him at some point in the last few days. Zey crossed the room, crawled onto the bed, and pulled me into his arms. This embrace wasn't sexual—it was so much more. We drew each other close, grieving silently for what would never be.

I held on to my dagger even as I clung to Zey, my knuckles going white with how tightly I was gripping it. It was the only thing making me feel like I had any fight left in me.

○ ○ ○

The dress Abraxos's people put me in wasn't my usual style, but I had to admit it was pretty. It was all shades of purple, its shimmery, gauzy fabric cinched at the waist and slits far too high up to conceal a dagger. I would've been irritated if I couldn't summon one with barely a thought.

The contouring done by an expert makeup artist made me look like a completely different person, which was good because my gods-damned hair was still pink.

As we approached the portal, I kicked myself again for forgetting to ask the guards to get me some hair dye. I'd had three whole days to do it, and I'd been so distracted by Z's D that I completely forgot. It was a good thing that most people with us wore bright colors or even had crazy hues in their hair. At least I didn't stand out.

Zey's hand wrapped around mine, and I squeezed it tightly. This was the first hurdle—getting us back to Earth unnoticed.

While it had taken a team of people several hours to disguise me and make me look like I fit in with a bunch of insanely beautiful creatures, Zey had simply picked an angel who would not be coming with us and shifted to look like him—complete with iridescent wings and everything. Typical.

He was a little shorter and Black, with short dreadlocks, but I knew it was him. I could feel him nearby, regardless of what he looked like.

My soul recognized his.

Which was something to worry about later because we were passing through the portal.

Abraxos had timed things well. There was a lot of traffic from Celestia/Soleil to Earth, angels and demons heading to the ball at Sea and Serpentine. As we stepped through, I did my best to look casual and carefree while scanning the scene.

The area was crawling with portal guards, but they were clearly run ragged by the rush. Our group was so large, it doubled the crowd passing through. Several people in our group were half-drunk already and causing a ruckus, laughing and joking and completely ignoring the guards.

Several guards glared at us and barked instructions.

Zey ruffled his wings and pulled me into his side, turning so he was shielding me from view. At the front of our group, Abraxos was speaking with the guards, his voice barely carrying over the noise.

After a few tense moments, they let our group pass. They were probably just not in the mood to deal with Abraxos's entitled, pompous attitude, which I was sure he was exaggerating just for the occasion. I'd bet my favorite dagger he even asked "do you know who I am?" at one point.

Once we were clear of the guards and past the netting, a few of the angels took off, flying ahead. The rest of us piled into several carriages. There were no horses or other animals in sight, or even any of the equipment you'd expect to see at the front of a carriage to attach it to a horse. They all took off at the same time anyway, powered by some kind of magic.

We were in a carriage with two humans and a shifter of some kind. Abraxos had been ignoring us since we left his prison—sorry! *Manor*—which was totally fine by me.

The trek through the rainforest to the dock was much faster than it had been going the other way on foot. We crowded into a large boat and sped down the river. We slowed almost to a stop at the edge of Sea and Serpentine territory, and I felt the distinctive barrier magic press against my skin as we passed through. There were dozens of mermaids in the water and shapes moving in the tree line on shore. But those in the boat and those in the water were all Sea and Serpentine members and recognized each other as such. Zey and I stayed out of sight, and they waved us through.

At the dock in Macapá, we disembarked and got into more of those horseless carriages. In procession, they ferried us through the bustling streets of the city and right through the gates of the Sea and Serpentine headquarters.

The main building came into view as we passed manicured gardens and an obscene number of water features. It practically looked like it was glowing with all the magical lights decorating the building and the surrounding area. Music wafted out as we rounded the massive fountain in the middle of the circular drive and stopped. People dressed in elaborate, stunning evening wear were talking on the drive or making their way in.

I tapped into my power briefly, triple checking that the Onuei was still there. The ribbons twirled out and straight to the same room on the third floor.

Zey gave me a meaningful look, like he knew what I was doing.

I nodded. "It's still in there."

As we rolled up, he whipped his head around and looked hard at the front of the building.

"So are my friends, apparently," he muttered.

"Shit. How many?" We knew there was a high probability that the Lineg Legion would try to grab the Onuei when we did, but it was still an unwelcome element that could prove to be disastrous.

"Around sixty. Maybe more."

I closed my eyes and released a tense breath through my nose. That was a lot. More than we'd anticipated.

"Will they sense you here?" I'd floated the idea of going in alone for this reason, but he'd shut it down immediately. Apparently, we were doing this together or not at all.

"Unless they specifically focus on me, no. One good thing about so many being here—they won't notice one more."

"Let's hope so."

The carriages stopped and everyone piled out, jovially heading towards the entrance like we owned the place.

Abraxos was causing a scene, as planned. Though technically part of the House of Sea and Serpentine, he hardly ever made any contribution or attended events. It wasn't an obvious House choice for an angel, but Abraxos was nothing if not cunning, and that made him fit right in. I was sure that Asbesta had a good reason for allowing him to be part of the House she ruled and to take such a liberal approach to his participation.

Most of the other guests openly glared at him. He was not well liked by either the angels or the demons of his own realm, and clearly not by the members of his own House either.

His mere appearance at this ball was enough to be a distraction, but of course, he was making sure to act as sanctimonious as I was sure he felt anyway.

Zey and I stayed close to the others as they ignored the House officials' half-hearted attempts to stop us from going in. I had no idea how much Abraxos's people knew of who we were or what we were doing here, but they all crowded us in the middle and swept us along with them—straight into the building. So they must've known something.

I caught a brief snippet of an argument between

Abraxos and the guards as we passed. The guards were trying to tell Abraxos he couldn't just bring all these dirty humans into the House headquarters, and Abraxos insisted he couldn't possibly do without his servants for an entire night. Clearly hoping to avoid a scene, the guards let us through, scoffing at the idea of humans roaming their precious space.

I could hardly believe it had been this easy and momentarily questioned my decision to go to Abraxos for help, to make a bargain that made my skin crawl. Maybe Zey and I could've done this ourselves.

But looking around at all the people present and how our group fit in while also drawing some disapproving looks, I knew it was Abraxos and his reputation that had done most of the heavy lifting here.

No point dwelling on it now anyway. It was done, and I was determined to make sure it wouldn't be wasted.

I'd been to more events like this than I could count. Most were hosted by Spirit and Sapphire, but I'd attended plenty others too. Usually I was there as a representative of my House, but at times I was also assigned as security to a high-ranking member or had a secret mission. Since the Great Sacrifice, the Houses were technically at peace, but they all had their alliances and rivalries. My particular set of skills ensured Spirit and Sapphire was aware of magical assets the others may have in their possession—or if and where they moved. For instance, if someone was in possession of a large amount of gabbro, we might wonder why they were stockpiling the powerful imbuing stone. And if another House happened to suddenly be in possession of that gabbro, we'd know a trade or deal had been done.

It was no surprise to see plenty of people who were not members of Sea and Serpentine in attendance. Most of Sea and Serpentine's members spent a majority of their time in water, so Asbesta liked to throw a ball once a year under the guise of diplomatic relations. We all knew that it was really just to remind the other Houses that Sea and Serpentine was here and was powerful—and it was a good opportunity for gathering intel and occasionally some light subterfuge.

If the other Houses refused the invitation, it would be a diplomatic incident and likely lead to war, so they all sent representatives, if not their leaders. I wasn't too worried about being spotted by passing acquaintances from other Houses or my own. But Lowell was there, along with two other high-ranking members of Spirit and Sapphire who knew me well, even if we weren't close friends.

"Let's get a drink," I said, turning my back to them and starting to head towards the bar. Zey wrapped an arm around my waist and pulled me in a different direction.

"Let's dance first," he insisted, leading me to the dance floor and turning me into his chest.

"What the hell are you doing?" I gritted out as I placed a hand on his shoulder and let him lead me through a waltz.

"*There are too many Vuulectians near the bar,*" he said telepathically while his face remained neutral. "*I need to avoid getting too close to any of them.*"

"Well, there are people from my House over by the terrace," I whispered, leaning into him like I wanted to get intimate. The far wall of the spacious ballroom was lined in tall windows and French doors flung open to let the sweet air in. The terrace and gardens were beyond.

Zey breathed my hair in, his hand flexing at my waist. Images of all the depraved things we'd done together over the past few days flashed through my mind.

I forced them away, ignoring the ache between my legs. I had to focus.

"We will work together to avoid them all, my . . ." he trailed off and spun me with a flourish. I frowned but was distracted by how well he danced. I wondered if they did that where he was from or if it was just an intuitive learning thing.

As we glided over the dance floor, I looked around, taking in as much information as possible. Where and how many exits there were, who looked like security pretending to be partygoers, who I recognized and needed to steer clear of.

With every spin Zey guided me through, I glanced at the spot near the French doors where Lowell and the others were. He looked bored out of his mind and was frequently tugging at the collar of his starched shirt. He hated these things even more than I did, and nothing made him itchier to shift than a button-up.

His eyes flicked around the room as he took a sip from a dainty champagne glass that looked ridiculous in his big hand. My heart leapt into my throat as he looked right at me, but his gaze passed over me, and his attention was drawn back to the conversation he was in.

I wasn't sure if I was more relieved or disappointed. I missed the big guy, and I just wanted a hug from my best friend and a night of drinking beer and talking through all the crazy-ass shit that had been going on. But I knew if he touched me with a ten-foot pole right now he'd be in serious trouble, and I didn't want that.

Suddenly, the lights dimmed and the music changed. Everyone turned to look at the wall of French doors as performers streamed in. There were angels flying over everyone's heads, their iridescent wings catching the light from the chandeliers; mermaids waded into the decorative pool in the center of the room and started synchronized swimming; a water fae manipulated the water, sending it flying about the room and dancing with the angels above, tying everything together into one cohesive performance.

The crowd pressed closer as the performers started to spread through the room, incorporating the guests in their display.

Zey and I didn't even need to talk telepathically or share a look. We knew this was a perfect opportunity to sneak off. Hand-in-hand, we drifted to the back of the room and slipped into the foyer.

There were two Sea and Serpentine guys at the front doors, chatting and standing around with nothing to do now that all the guests were inside. The front doors were wide open though, so Zey and I crossed the space as silently as we could and climbed the grand staircase.

Hallways branched off the first landing in both directions. They were dark and empty, the doors to offices and other rooms shut. But we needed to get to the third floor. I'd made Zey memorize the route to the Onuei—just in case things fell apart.

A light, female laugh drifted down the stairs, followed by the sound of footsteps. Two mermaids were descending the steps, their gowns floating behind them. I yanked Zey into a doorway and pulled him down into a kiss.

He pressed in closer, bracketing me in against the door with his body and his wings.

"Is this really the best time for sexual gratification, Sky?" he said in my mind, his voice teasing. He knew very well what I was doing and was playing along more than willingly, judging by the hardness nudging against my hip.

Unable to respond, I sucked his bottom lip into my mouth and bit down just a little too hard.

He grunted, the sound something between surprise and pleasure.

"Seriously?" one of the women said. "Get a room."

"So juvenile," the other one added.

I glanced over Zey's shoulder and breathed a sigh of relief to see their backs to us. They'd made their judgy comments and were rushing away.

As soon as they were out of sight, we broke apart and rushed up the stairs, all the way to the top floor.

The landing was clear. It was quiet up here, the sounds of music muffled and barely audible.

I checked one corridor—empty. By the time I turned to look down the opposite one, it was already too late.

"Hey! You can't be up here!" A guard was marching towards us. He was a shifter, probably an aquatic animal judging by his House choice. His purposeful steps ate up the distance.

The "we snuck away from the party to hook up" ruse was not going to work with this dude. I really didn't want to fight a dolphin or whatever he was. Shifters of all kinds were stupid strong. Even if we won the fight, it would certainly draw the attention of others.

Sighing, I summoned a gun.

Before I could raise it, Zey stepped around me and took several leisurely steps towards the guard. He'd shifted, no longer resembling the Black angel whose image he'd copied at Abraxos's house.

"Did you hear me? You need to—" The guard came to an abrupt stop a few feet away, standing taller.

"Need to . . ." Zey tilted his head and raised his eyebrows. He'd shifted into Philatanus—a demon and Asbesta's second in command. He had a solid, almost stocky build and a strong brow.

"Apologies, sir. I didn't realize it was you," the guard said in a much lower tone.

Zey just grunted, adjusted his leathery wings, and looked at me over his shoulder, effectively dismissing the guy.

"This way." He held his hand out, ushering me down the corridor. I kept the gun tucked into the folds of my dress and moved to his side at a measured pace. He placed a hand on my lower back, and we wandered away from the guard without incident.

I'd spotted Philatanus downstairs at the party, but I hadn't said anything to Zey. I had no idea how he knew to shift into him, but I was glad he did.

When we rounded the corner, we sped up, and Zey shifted into his chosen human form. I smiled despite myself. I'd missed his stupid face.

We went right to the door we knew the Onuei was behind.

I reached for the handle.

A whoosh of wind hit my bare shoulder, the sound of wings filling the empty space as a hand clamped around my wrist.

CHAPTER 17

Reflexively, I twisted and shoved the gun up under the chin of . . .

"Abraxos?" I hissed.

Stepping around me, Zey punched him in the face.

"Ow," Abraxos deadpanned. "Was that really necessary? And you can lower the gun now, Sky, darling."

With a sigh, I lowered my weapon.

"My bad." Zey shrugged. "Didn't realize it was you."

"You punched me *after* Sky said my name," Abraxos pointed out.

"Children," I snapped. "Can we please focus?"

I reached for the handle again, but Abraxos wrapped an arm around my waist and lifted me away from the door, setting me down on his other side.

"What the hell?" I seethed at the same time as Zey said, "Put her down."

"Unless you'd like to bring several guards and possibly even Asbesta up here, allow me to open the door." Abraxos looked between us like we were children he was teaching a lesson to.

"The doors are spelled?" I shook my head, berating myself for forgetting that possibility.

"They are indeed. Only certain members of Sea and Serpentine can open the doors on the third floor."

"And they gave *you* access?" Zey scoffed.

"Yes. I am a very important and handsome individual." He flashed us a grin. Then he reached out, produced a small vial of what looked like plain water, and poured it on the door handle. The water was clearly not plain, because it slithered into the lock, and the click of it unlocking brought a self-satisfied smile to Abraxos's face before he opened the door with a flourish. "I also stole this *key* from a tipsy mermaid before following you two upstairs."

"So, it would've been fine had I tried to open the door?" I gave him a withering look and shoved past him into the room.

"No. The doors are indeed spelled to members of Sea and Serpentine—they all are. But these ones require a special *key* as well." He waved the delicate vial—now full of water once more—in front of my face. I batted him away.

"Sky, it's not here." Zey's worried words drew my attention. He'd closed the door behind us and was looking around the room with a deep frown.

It looked like a space that was being used for storage, but it wasn't cluttered and messy. There was a lot of stuff, but the boxes were stacked neatly, the several shelves organized though bursting with books and other items.

I rushed to the corner where my power had shown me the Onuei. The necklace was sitting in a glass cabinet, right where I thought it would be. The room wasn't huge—Zey should've been able to feel it at this proximity.

I looked over my shoulder at him. He came to stand next to me as I opened the cabinet and took it out. It was an old-fashioned style of necklace with many pieces of highly polished serpentine set into intricate silver settings. It was exactly what my ability had shown me when I searched for it.

Zey glanced at it, then back at me and shook his head.

"This better not be some kind of trick to avoid giving me what we agreed on," Abraxos said, a clear warning in his tone.

"Shh," I hushed him, batting him away as I closed my eyes.

When I'd first searched for the Onuei, the image of the necklace in this room had been so clear. And when we pulled up to the building earlier, I'd checked to make sure it was still here, and the ribbons in my mind had shot up to the exact same room and that exact piece of ugly jewelry.

I gave my power all my attention as I let the ribbons unfurl, seeking the Onuei with more intention.

They stretched and floated all the way back down the three flights of stairs, through the foyer, into the ballroom full of people and . . .

"It's downstairs," I said, frowning at the necklace in my hands. "It was here when we arrived. This doesn't make sense."

"You're telling me we went through all this effort for nothing?" Abraxos drawled.

"Where is it, Sky?" Zey asked, ignoring him.

"It's around the neck of a mermaid who's currently dancing with someone. It looks exactly like this." I held the necklace up. "It was right here. Someone must've . . ."

"Someone stole it before we could." Zey finished the thought for me.

"Someone with access to the very secure third-floor

rooms," Abraxos pointed out. "And they took the trouble of replacing it with a good decoy."

The three of us shared a loaded look. Whoever had done this had to have been a member of Sea and Serpentine *and* had access to one of those water keys *and* knew exactly what they were after so they could bring the fake.

This was not good.

Getting down the stairs was much easier than going up. We breezed past the guard on the third floor, then past another one on the second—who knew where he'd been when we were going up. *Naughty, naughty.*

Back in the ballroom, we nibbled on finger food and scanned the dance floor over flutes of champagne. Abraxos was sticking to us like a barnacle. I was starting to get the sense that he was enjoying this almost as much as he was determined to get the Orb of Sinne. It was all a big game to him.

I let my ability do the work for us and followed the ribbons to what I was looking for. The woman had left the dance floor and was hovering near the bar with a few others. She wore a dress with a high neckline and exposed back, no jewelry in sight. But I was certain that necklace was tucked under her dress.

"Over by the bar," I mumbled, leaning into Zey like I was tipsy. "In the pink dress."

Abraxos shuffled in closer to my back, his hand caressing my waist. Zey and I both stiffened. Plenty of people were getting amorous with more than one person, but neither of us liked Abraxos being so damn close and personal.

"Jadika? Why would she steal from her own House?" he whispered, his mouth far too close to my neck.

"That's not Jadika," Zey said. "That's a Vuulectian. And I can feel the Onuei on her. It's obvious now that I'm looking for it."

"Sneaky little shape-shifters." Abraxos chuckled before dragging his nose up my neck.

I went to elbow him in the stomach, but he disappeared before I could move.

He wove through the crowd, spinning dancers and sipping drinks, then discarding them almost full as he went.

I swore under my breath as he went right up to the Vuulectian disguised as Jadika the mermaid.

"What the fuck does he think he's doing?" Zey gritted out.

"I'm sure he thinks he's helping." I sighed. "Come on."

I tugged him closer, and we mingled in the crowd, dodging Vuulectians and acquaintances while pretending to enjoy the party.

Annoying as he was, I could see what Abraxos was doing. If the Lineg Legion wanted to get away unnoticed, they had to be careful. The one pretending to be Jadika couldn't exactly ignore a member of the House of Sea and Serpentine without drawing attention.

It was not like we could come up with another plan anyway, so we may as well help with this one.

When Abraxos started leading Jadika towards the foyer, Zey and I headed in the same direction.

"He's trying to get her alone," I murmured.

"The others will follow," Zey said. There was no way they'd leave the Onuei unprotected.

There were more people mingling in the foyer now,

some leaving, others just taking a breather from the increasingly rowdy party.

I giggled and took Zey's hand, pulling him towards the back of the building. He played along, jogging to catch up and tickle me. I glanced over my shoulder to make sure Abraxos was following, and he caught my eye for the briefest moment as he led Jadika out of the main ball room.

Rounding a corner, I opened the first door I found. It was a service corridor, staff rushing up and down, the kitchen just visible at the other end.

It was too busy, so I shut the door and moved on.

We rushed past the bathrooms, and Zey reached for the last door. It opened to a dark sitting room, much more plainly decorated than the rest of the house, but comfortable. There were a few couches, bookshelves, and a dying fire in the hearth between two French doors.

It was probably a staff room, but they were all clearly run off their feet.

We closed the door halfway and waited.

In the next moment, Abraxos came around the same corner gesticulating ostentatiously while "Jadika" looked bored next to him.

I opened the door wider, making sure to remain in the shadows, and he sped up, shuffling her right inside.

I caught a glimpse of several people coming around the corner as I closed the door.

"We don't have much time." I turned to find Zey holding the woman by the throat, a zap held to her side. She was beautiful. Her black hair hung down her back in a thick braid and shimmered purple when it shifted, and her warm brown skin looked so smooth and hydrated that it practically glowed. Her dark eyes were wide with fear and shock.

"Won't need much. Doendru here isn't going to call out

to our friends, telepathically or out loud, are you?" he said menacingly. "As long as the others can feel her and the Onuei close by, they'll stay where they are.

The other Vuulectian stared at him with a hard expression, but those big, wide eyes still showed her fear.

Abraxos leaned against the wall by the door, looking bored.

I rushed forward, reached under the front of her dress, and yanked the necklace off.

The Vuulectian turned those expressive eyes up to Zey. "You would let a human handle something so precious?" She sounded outraged.

"You would let the ancient magic of the Onuei be perverted like this? Keep them from our one True Leader while our people are lied to? Do not act outraged with me, Doendru."

"What are you talking about?" Doendru looked confused. "The Lineg Legion are trying to get the Onuei back home to their rightful place. *You* are the one trying to steal them for your own benefit."

Zey laughed darkly. "Is this the lie they're spreading? And you believe them?"

He sounded a little hurt. I wanted to punch Doendru.

"Why would they lie?" She sounded uncertain.

"Why would *I* lie?" Zey threw back. "You've known me your entire life. I swore to protect the True Leader and the Onuei with my own life. I watched Silovisuvinoucraptiles and two of his disgraceful Lineg Legion conspirators *murder* our beloved Leader. I barely made it out alive."

"Touching as this family reunion is," Abraxos drawled from his dark spot by the door. "You have what you were after. My end of the bargain is fulfilled, and I really must be on my way."

He looked at me expectantly. I wrapped my hand around the necklace tighter.

The door to the sitting room opened, drawing all our eyes as a demon man stepped inside and closed it behind him.

"Sky Serpell." He gave me a tight smile and glanced at Zey. "And friend. Why am I not surprised?"

I glanced at the door, hoping the Vuulectians on the other side hadn't seen anything to send them running in here when he'd come in.

Philatanus was a prominent member of the House of Sea and Serpentine, Asbesta's second. Zey had shifted into him to get past that guard earlier, and it was a little unsettling to see the actual man step into the room with us. Philatanus had been heavily involved with House business for decades before I was even born. We'd met plenty of times; I'd always thought of him as a reserved, if somewhat cold man, more interested in numbers than politics.

I was pretty sure I could take him.

Stuffing his hands into his pockets, he turned his attention to Abraxos. "I suppose this explains your attendance tonight. Working with wanted fugitives." He shook his head and tsked. "I don't think Asbesta would want someone she can't trust in Sea and Serpentine."

Abraxos chuckled, sauntering forward casually, his magnificent wings shimmering in the light from the fire while Philatanus's seemed to almost disappear in the shadows.

"Like I give a shit about being in your little Earth club." Abraxos all but rolled his eyes. "Not like you do. I wonder, can Asbesta trust someone who's working with the Vuulectians to steal a precious artifact? I'm assuming she's unaware of this little . . . *alliance*? Otherwise, there'd be no need to place a decoy in its place, would there?"

Philatanus was working with the Vuulectians? I shouldn't have been surprised—I'd pretty much seen it all when it came to House politics. But why?

The question was at the tip of my tongue, but ultimately it didn't matter. It was either for personal gain or it was House politics at play. Perhaps he'd struck a deal to help them get the Onuei in exchange for an exclusive alliance with Sea and Serpentine. If he pulled it off, he'd have the favor of Asbesta, more power in the House. But he was doing it secretly because if he failed, no one had to know.

"Anyway," Philatanus turned to Zey and Doendru, "why haven't you used your . . ." He pointed to his head, indicating telepathy.

Doendru glanced down to where Zey was still holding the zap to her side and gave him a 'duh' look.

I summoned the gun I'd stashed under an accent chair in that storage room upstairs and pointed it at Philatanus. "Don't even think about it." I didn't think a gun could kill a demon, but I was pretty sure it would hurt like a bitch all the same.

He raised his hands slowly. "No need for this to get messy. Just hand the necklace over and you can leave without anyone else knowing you were even here."

"No," Zey and I barked at the same time.

"*Anyway.*" Abraxos sounded exasperated. In the blink of an eye, he shot forward, grabbed Philatanus, and twisted so he held the other man's back to his chest. A sharp blade the size of my forearm glinted in the fading light of the fire, held to Philatanus's throat.

"The location of the Orb, Sky. *Now*," he demanded, his patience clearly at an end.

Philatanus's eyes widened, his mouth falling open in horror as he stared at me. "The Orb of Sinne? What have you done?" he breathed. The demon's reaction had me worried all over again about letting it fall into Abraxos's hands. I had no idea what that damn orb did, but I now had an idea of just how powerful it was.

I moved the gun from Philatanus to Abraxos and back again, uncertain whom to aim for. I may have pointed a weapon at Philatanus myself, but I was never going to kill the guy. Maim him a little, maybe bust a kneecap. I wasn't willing to let people die if I could avoid it. I was positive Abraxos didn't have the same qualms though. He would absolutely murder whomever stood in his way.

Abraxos pressed the blade harder, drawing blood as the other man winced.

"OK! Fuck," I gritted out. "From Lapsus Manor, you need to go to the other side of the crater and keep going straight for a very long time. When you come to a copse of trees—"

"You lie!" He cut me off, digging the sharp blade a little harder into Philatanus's throat. "Nothing grows in Dead Man's Land."

"She speaks the truth. I've seen it," Philatanus rushed out. He looked disgusted to be confirming my words, but he also wanted to live.

"In the trees, there's a door of crystal set into a frame of volcanic rock. The Orb of Sinne is through that door. That's all I know."

"If you're lying to me, I will come back and get what I was promised, and it will not be pleasant for you, Sky," Abraxos said calmly.

The look on Zey's face was murderous.

"That's all I saw. I promise," I assured him.

"Very well then." He slashed the blade across Philatanus's throat, making the rest of us gasp in surprise. The large blade dug deeper with ease until it went straight through. Blood gushed everywhere, and then the head toppled off the body. Philatanus was dead in seconds, discarded on the worn carpet at Abraxos's feet. He stepped over the body like it was an inconvenient piece of trash.

"Why?" Doendru asked, sounding shaken and confused.

"He knew too much." Abraxos shrugged as he opened one of the French doors.

"Where the fuck are you going?" I demanded. We still had the little issue of a horde of Vuulectians to deal with.

"Our business is done. I agreed to help you attain your necklace. You never said anything about getting out of Sea and Serpentine headquarters. Good luck, Sky Serpell." With one last scowl in Zey's direction, he stepped into the night and flew off, the sound of his flapping wings fading fast.

"Son of a bitch," Zey spat, his whole body radiating tension.

Doendru made a startled sound of fear, shaking where she stood and looking around at everything with wide eyes.

"Please don't hurt me, Zey," she cried. *Too loud.* I glanced at the door. "Please don't kill me!"

Shit. They definitely would've heard that.

Zey was looking at her like he was horrified and hurt that she thought he'd kill her.

Time's up.

I jammed a chair under the door handle and rushed

over to them. A banging noise came from the door, the Vuulectians trying to get in.

Doendru yelled, now crying and clearly freaking out.

Zey was murmuring something, looking between the door and her, trying to get her to calm down.

I yanked the zap from his hand and stabbed it into the side of Doendru's neck. At the jolt of electricity, she dropped to the ground, passed out.

Wood splintered—they were almost through the door.

I grabbed Zey's hand and pulled him through the open French doors.

We ran into the gardens that surrounded the house as more shouts erupted around us. It was dark and hard to see, but Zey snapped out of whatever was going on with him and took the lead. I guessed he could see in the dark, or he'd shifted his eyes so they could, because he took my hand and maneuvered us around fountains and garden beds.

"Which way, Sky?" he rushed out.

We were running away from the house and were bound to hit the fence at some point, but then what? I had no idea if it was guarded or magically protected.

We were so fucking fucked!

One quick glance behind us told me there were several people racing after us. They were going in multiple directions though, so the darkness was helping at least a little bit.

Not with the Vuulectians though—now that they knew Zey was here, they were locked on him and heading straight for us. The two Onuei in our possession probably didn't help either.

A big, hulking form came rushing at us from the side, appearing from behind some hedge, too late to avoid.

Zey shoved me to the side and threw a punch.

The other guy dodged it, and I realized I knew him.

"Lowell?" I called, breathing hard. I knew his mannerisms, the way he moved his large frame way faster than most expected.

"Sky?" he called back, and Zey relaxed marginally. "Let's move."

I didn't hesitate. I trusted Lowell with my life and ran after him as he ducked behind the hedge and led the way back to where he came from.

With Vuulectians hot on our heels and more and more shouts coming from the building, we reached the edge of the property.

A guard lay prone on the ground, relieved of his weapons and unconscious. There was a hole in the fence behind him, and Lowell helped us through before following us.

"This way." He jogged away from the main road to the quieter streets behind the House of Sea and Serpentine headquarters.

"What are you doing?" I hissed, smacking his arm as we kept pace with him. "Why are you going around knocking guards out?"

"Spotted you when you arrived. Figured you might need a few exit options. Looks like I was right." Even in this dire situation, he managed a small, satisfied grin.

I wanted to hug him. He'd saved my ass again. I'd done the same for him so many times too. We'd stopped keeping count years ago.

"You are going to get into so much shit. I can't be responsible for ruining your life too." I groaned.

"I don't know what you're talking about, traitor," he said, stopping at the entrance to a parking area and pulling a set of keys out of his pocket. "I saw you attack that guard and escape through the fence and went chasing after you.

I'm a big guy and a good fighter, but I couldn't take two of you, and unfortunately, you knocked me the fuck out before stealing my keys and jumping on my bike that's parked right over there," he pointed at the corner of the lot, "and I didn't see which way you went."

I took the keys from him and pulled him into a quick hug. My heart was bursting at how much he was willing to risk for me.

"The Vuulectians will still be able to track us, but this will be a good head start. Thank you," Zey said earnestly, and I could hear the note of respect in his tone.

"Thank you," I rushed out as I pulled back.

Lowell just gave me a firm nod and turned to Zey. "Hope you've got a powerful swing buddy, because this needs to be believable."

No time to waste, Zey shifted. His shoulders widened and he gained a few extra inches, his clothing straining against the extra bulk.

"Oh man, that's fucking weird." Lowell chuckled, wide-eyed as he stared at a carbon copy of himself.

Zey reared back and punched my best friend in the head—hard. I winced, then helped him to lower his bulk to the ground gently.

We ran to the bike, my mind working in overdrive to think of where we could possibly go to get away from what I was sure were now dozens of people coming after us.

CHAPTER 18

One of the perks of my job, and my side-hustle, was all the travel and the many things I got to learn. Like how to find a witch who was willing to open a portal for the right price, for example.

Zey maneuvered the motorcycle with expert ease, weaving through the narrow, busy streets of Macapá. I pointed where I wanted him to turn, and he moved at a frightening speed, somehow still managing to not hit any people or inanimate objects.

Between directions, I was keeping my eye out for our pursuers, but they'd been nowhere in sight since we blew through the border of Sea and Serpentine territory and into No Man's Land several blocks ago.

I navigated us around a few more turns, then gestured for Zey to stop. We parked the motorcycle in an alleyway.

"We don't have much time." Zey was looking over my shoulder, feeling out the Vuulectians after us.

"Yeah, yeah. What else is new?" I grumbled and scanned the busy street as we walked. The buildings here were crumbling, held together by magic and duct tape, the area a bustling mash-up of bars, street food vendors, and markets selling everything from burner phones to viloss dust.

I spotted a young fae leaning in the doorway of one of the rowdier establishments and smoking a pipe that produced green smoke. Usually, I didn't like to get heavy-handed, preferring to get my information through more diplomatic means. But I simply didn't have time for that.

I marched right up to the fae, giving him a sultry grin. His eyes quickly scanned my scantily clad body, and he smirked after blowing out a big plume of green smoke. Once I was in his space, I summoned my favorite blade, shoved him against the door, and held the blade to his neck.

"Tell me where I can find a witch to open a portal. Now," I demanded. His eyes bugged out, and he started trembling. A string of high-pitched Portuguese came tumbling out of his mouth, wisps of green smoke trailing out after.

I growled in frustration, ready to threaten him some more, but Zey appeared next to us.

His hand gently wrapped around my wrist, but his gaze was fixed on the fae as he said something in what I was sure was perfect Portuguese. His voice was low, soothing, and the fae nodded, then said some more things I didn't understand while pointing at something across the street.

"Let's go." Zey tugged on my wrist, and I released the terrified man.

I followed Zey across the street and into a narrow one-way lane.

"Was the violence really necessary?" Zey arched a brow at me.

"Yes," I huffed and tucked the blade into the holster at my thigh.

Zey chuckled. "Our frightened friend informed me there is a powerful crone witch in the building on the corner with the purple door."

There were fewer people as we walked further away from the main strip, the buildings quiet or boarded up.

I let Zey lead me along as I clutched the second Onuei in my hand and concentrated on seeking out the third one.

At the next intersection, we came upon a purple door. I knocked firmly.

A female voice shouted something from the inside.

"She says they are closed for the day," Zey translated.

"Tell her we'll pay her just for opening the door," I said.

The faded purple door swung open before Zey could convey my message in Portuguese.

A woman in jean shorts and a loose shirt opened the door. She was about my age, her dark hair piled on her head in a messy bun, her striking eyes narrowed.

She looked us up and down as she said in accented English, "You must be in a hell of a clusterfuck if you're offering to pay me just for opening the door."

"Just on a very tight deadline." I gave her a thin smile. "We need a portal. Only a few minutes of your time. Name your price."

She pursed her lips, but after a moment, stepped aside so we could enter.

"Hurry." Zey looked out the little window next to the door.

"Where to?" the crone asked.

"Cairo. How much?"

"Fae hair. Twenty strands."

Shit. I only had three in my possession. I had all kinds of spells and potions—some rare, most pretty common—the kind of things used for day-to-day living expenses. But a witch had no use for these things when she could make them herself. I had several vials of shifter blood, a couple of angel feathers, and only three strands of fae hair.

I offered her all I had.

She shook her head. "All common enough in this area, but not many fae here. I need the strands or no portal."

"They're closing in," Zey reminded me unhelpfully.

"Is there nothing else you need? Please. There must be something outside the common trade items." I wasn't above begging in a life-or-death situation.

"Nothing you have, I assure you," she scoffed.

"Try me!" I must've looked crazed, imploring her to just fucking work with me here.

"The only other thing I have in short supply is *ngarat-ngat*." She reached into a basket sitting on the table behind her and pulled out a dark red, withered piece of what looked like bark. "Hard to get. Only grows in the Philippines. Very expensive. One whole dried petal for a portal." She said it with tight smile, like that was the end of that and we should leave now.

"Done," I said, and she chuckled in disbelief. I didn't have the luxury of asking for permission, so I just reached out and grabbed the shriveled plant. With the energetic signature in my palm and a location already in mind, I sent my ribbons out with urgency. They did my bidding as usual, and I avoided some of the closer specimens, not willing to steal something that was clearly expensive. Instead, I focused on the Philippines, and my power quickly found the plant in the wilderness and wrapped itself around it tightly. I *pulled*.

An entire flower appeared in my arms. I was in a rush and didn't have the time to concentrate on summoning only a single petal. But I kind of wished I had. The thing was huge and heavy, and I needed both arms to keep it from flopping onto the ground.

"Portal! Now!" I barked as I set the weird red plant on the table.

The witch snapped out of her shock and quickly got to work. She was clearly powerful and highly skilled. I'd never seen someone conjure a magic basin so fast. Her lips moved rapidly as she muttered the spell, and I grabbed my knife in preparation for the sacrifice.

The witch glanced up and nodded that she was ready.

Zey's hand wrapped around my wrist, stopping me from cutting myself. "I will provide the sacrifice."

"Zey, we don't even know if—"

He cut me off by shifting his head into its original faceless form and *reaching his hand right into it*. He plucked one of the ethereal little lights that seemed to float in his head and pulled it out. It must've hurt, because his skin did that jagged rippling thing, but he didn't make any sound as he dropped the piece of himself into the bowl.

The witch was staring at us with wide eyes, but she kept chanting. She was going to have some stories to tell her friends over drinks after our little visit.

Her eyes glowed white, and she threw the shimmering magic bowl into the air. It transformed and exploded with light, turning into a portal.

"You may want to open one of these for yourself," Zey said as we stepped up to the swirling, powerful magic. "You're about to have some very unpleasant company."

The crone threw her head back and laughed. "I don't let anyone drive me out of my home—especially *filhos da mãe* brand new to this world."

"Thank you!" I smiled as we stepped through the portal. I had to admire her strength and power.

"Thank *you*! I am in your debt."

There was a loud bang on the door, but the portal closed behind us before we could see what happened next. I really hoped she'd be OK. I liked her.

We went from one bustling, dodgy neighborhood to another. There was a different language being spoken, and the sun was only just rising over one of the busiest No Man's Land cities in the world, but the general vibe was the same.

I turned to Zey and found him observing our surroundings with a very sour look on his face.

"You good?" I nudged him and we started moving through the crowd. I wasn't sure where we were heading yet, but we couldn't just stand around holding our dicks in our hands.

"It's so . . ." he looked around and even up to the sky. "Dry," he finally finished.

"Yeah, well, that's why they call it the desert. I knew you were going to hate it." I chuckled.

"Ugh. I don't like it."

"Don't worry. We'll keep you nice and hydrated." I took his hand and gave him a reassuring squeeze. At the contact, my power surged through me so strongly that I stumbled. That had never happened to me before. It was like the magic was demanding I pay attention and go get the final Onuei. Touching Zey—and by extension the two Onuei he had stashed away in his pockets—coupled with the fact we were now closer to the last Onuei had made it really easy to find. But my ability had never taken over like that before, had never surged through me without beckoning it.

"It's like something is forcing me to seek," I gritted out.

"The Onuei are close to being reunited. What do you see, Sky?" Zey held on to my hand and guided us into an alcove, out of the way of the busy foot traffic. The Onuei were a strange kind of magic, and when I thought about it, it did make sense that they'd have some level of sentience. Forced by inanimate objects to use my ability—rude.

I leaned my forehead against Zey's chest and focused on following the trail.

A thick, shimmering ribbon unfurled in my mind's eye, shooting out so fast it almost looked blurry. It traced a path directly into the desert. All I could see for miles and miles was golden sand and bright blue sky. I followed it until it became clear it was just going to keep showing me sand dunes and I got impatient. We needed to head into the desert. That much was very clear.

I looked up at Zey, and he gave me a small smile as he waited patiently for my directions. He'd wrapped his arms around my waist while I'd gone flying in my head. Relaxing into his embrace, I draped my own around his neck.

"We're gonna need a Jeep," I said before pulling his head down and kissing him firmly. I was suddenly aware that our time together was extremely limited. We could have the third Onuei by the end of the day. If everything went smoothly, this could all be over within a matter of days.

Nothing had gone smoothly so far though, so it would probably be difficult and frustrating and take forever. For the first time, I wasn't in a rush to get it all over with.

Digging my fingers into the back of his neck, I kissed him even harder.

He chuckled against my lips and pulled back.

"As much as I enjoy this, we should get going." He brushed my cheek with his thumb. "Time is—"

"Of the essence." I cut him off and forced myself to step out of his hold. "I know."

No point dwelling on it; I ignored the slight frown he gave me as I took off down the street.

It took us less than an hour to buy an old, but reliable vehicle equipped with sand tires and gather some supplies. I could summon most things we needed, but I had no idea how long we were going to be out there, so it was better to be prepared. Most of the back seat was taken up by massive jugs of water, as was the trunk. A small section had some food for me and a first aid kit.

We drove out of Cairo without any issues, and it wasn't long until the road cutting through the desert became more and more devoid of buildings, people, or animals. Once we'd been driving for a solid fifteen minutes without seeing anyone behind us or passing anyone going in the opposite direction, I pulled off the road.

There was probably a way to get closer to our destination using the roads, but I had a feeling it would end up taking us three times the amount of time to get there, and we'd still have to drive out into the barren landscape. So I decided to take the shortcut and point the vehicle directly towards where my power was pulling me to go.

We drove for hours with nothing but sand in any direction, the horizon constantly looking too far away. If it wasn't for the pull of my ability telling me we were getting closer to the third Onuei, I would've thought we were going around in circles. The heat, the monotone landscape, the absolute stillness of it all, was enough to drive a person crazy.

Zey was quiet, constantly taking small sips of water. I was starting to worry about him. I'd never seen him look so flat, like he wasn't feeling well. Considering his insatiable need for water, he probably wasn't.

We stopped only once, sitting in the sand in the shade

of the Jeep as I had a quick meal and we both guzzled some water. Then it was more hours and hours of driving.

The sun was low in the sky, painting the vastness before us and the patchy clouds in deep oranges and purples. It was throwing long shadows in the sand, making small sand dunes appear like mountains from far away. I figured we had maybe an hour of daylight left before the temperature plummeted along with the sun.

It felt like we were close, my power practically humming, but there was nothing nearby. I was starting to think the Onuei might be buried in the sand somewhere. It would be just my luck that it was buried deep in some undiscovered ancient tomb.

One problem at a time.

At first, I dismissed the shape in the distance as just another weird shadow and kept driving. But as the shape started to come into focus, I reflexively eased off the gas.

Zey leaned forward, looking intently at the same spot.

We were driving up to some kind of structure—if you could call it that. Even from this distance, it looked half destroyed. There was something white in front of it, flapping in the wind like a sheet drying on the line.

"Sense any of your buddies?" I asked.

"No." Zey shook his head.

"Good. Still . . ." We had no idea what we were walking into.

Zey hummed and reached behind us for a jug of water. He opened his mouth unnaturally wide and poured the entirety of it down his throat. Then he did the same with another two. I wished I had some kind of magic potion that I could drink and suddenly be at my best mentally and physically.

The closer we got, the more everything came into focus.

We were definitely looking at some kind of ruin. It was constructed of sandstone, and I could make out the remnants of a few walls, most of them half collapsed. One wall was still intact enough to have a small window in it, and a wide, arched doorway stood near the center of the front wall, but the rest of it was hardly more than rubble.

But it was that pristine white that held the most surprise.

"You seeing this?" I spoke low, keeping my eyes on the figure in white. "Or am I hallucinating?"

"You aren't. There's a woman." Zey confirmed that I wasn't losing it, but I wasn't sure if I should feel relieved.

A woman was indeed standing before the ruin, her long white dress flapping in the desert wind. We were close enough now to see that there was nothing in the ruin, let alone a place for someone to live. There was also no sign of a vehicle or any other living soul. It was entirely possible she'd gotten here using magical means but . . . why? Was she after the Onuei too? But why not just take it and go?

I stopped the Jeep a good ten feet away.

She had long, dark brown hair, half up to keep it out of her face. The dress was made of simple, light linen, draped on her body delicately, accompanied by a white lace choker at her neck. A wide, lace bracelet sat around her right wrist. A silver chain extended from the bracelet down the back of her hand to a pearlescent ring on her forefinger.

"I can feel the Onuei. It's very close," Zey whispered, scanning the area all around us.

"Same." It felt like she was standing right on top of it. Unless . . . surely she wasn't the Onuei?

Zey and I shared an uncertain look, then got out of the car. Tentatively, we started walking towards her.

She gave us a mild smile, like it was totally normal that

we were meeting in the literal middle of nowhere.

Just as I was about to say something, she spoke.

"Hurry. We don't have much time." Her voice was gentle, soft, but it carried to us easily. She turned and walked through the crumbling archway. As she passed under it, it was like a curtain was drawn back, and suddenly a whole other world was visible on the other side.

In complete contrast to the barren desert around us, the other side of the archway held a vibrant, verdant oasis. It was dense with lush plants and trees, water trickling off a small waterfall into a grotto, small birds flitting from branch to moss-covered branch.

For a moment, I thought she'd opened a portal, but there was no sparking magic around the edges, no strong power in the air. Clearly, she was a witch—a powerful one. Was this some kind of illusion?

I stopped at the threshold and grabbed Zey's wrist. She could trap us in whatever this was; she could be shielding a whole group of people ready to attack us.

"I'm not trying to hurt you, Sky," the woman said, just on the other side. "You've come for the Onuei." She shifted her gaze to Zey. "I'll give it to you freely."

She glanced behind us, the first sign of unease showing on her face. I narrowed my eyes.

Zey extracted his wrist from my grip and took my hand instead.

"We've come this far," he said, and I looked at him. I could see the determination in his eyes. He was right, of course. It was so close I could practically taste it. I wanted to give him what he wanted most—more than I wanted this mess to be over. I could admit that now.

With a sad smile, I nodded, and we stepped into the oasis together.

CHAPTER 19

The archway, along with any sign of the desert, disappeared. The air was mild and humid, and Zey took a deep breath. The moisture in the air must be real if he was feeling it. But how?

My hand hovered near the fighting knife at my thigh, ready to summon other weapons if needed.

"What is this place?" I asked. "Where are we?"

"This is a safe place." The woman smiled and sat on a low rock next to the grotto, running her fingers through the water.

"How do you know my name? Or what the Onuei even is?" I demanded.

"I admire your strength and confidence." She looked up at me with warring emotions on her face. It was strange to have someone gazing at you like they wanted your approval and thought you were an ignorant child at the same time. "But none of your questions are important right now. We don't have much time."

"You've said that already." Zey took a step closer to her,

dragging me along behind him reluctantly. "What do you mean?"

In answer, the woman got to her feet again and walked a few paces over to a tree. It was some kind of droopy tree, like a willow or something, with pieces of cloth and beads and charms hanging from every branch.

"You may remove the Onuei." She gestured to the tree, then clasped her hands in front of her.

Zey and I shared a look. With my power and his innate connection to the Onuei, it would be like taking, well, *anything* from a human. We moved forward together, my ability already seeking what I needed.

The woman held a hand up, palm out, and we stopped. "Only Zey. I'm sorry, Sky, but I need to be certain."

I shrugged and planted my hands on my hips as Zey approached the tree. He was more than capable of finding the Onuei at this proximity.

Zey walked slowly past the woman and ran his hands through the drooping foliage, making some of the trinkets chime as they collided.

The ribbons in my mind had already located what we were looking for, and I knew he wouldn't find it in the tree. Realizing the same thing, Zey turned and came to stand behind the woman. I smirked.

She tilted her head slightly, glancing at him over her shoulder as he reached up. Gently, he removed one of the ribbons that was tied into her hair. It was deep blue silk with delicate silver embroidery.

I chuckled despite myself. The ribbons in my mind's eye had been leading me to a literal ribbon. There was something kind of . . . poetic about that.

It was the final Onuei for sure. If my ability hadn't told me so, the awed, satisfied look on Zey's face would've.

My smile fell and I looked away. He had all he'd wanted since coming here, and before too long, he'd be gone.

I was a stupid idiot for letting myself get attached to a person who I knew very well was not going to be in my life for another week, let alone long-term.

"Thank you." Zey's earnest thanks drew my attention back to find the woman watching me closely.

She smiled. "It was my pleasure to keep it safe until you came for it."

It couldn't possibly be this easy.

"Why? Who the hell are you?" I barked. I may have been letting my complicated emotions out on the woman who was turning out to be completely harmless.

"Because it was the right thing to do. And my name is Emmaline," she answered simply. "I could feel the ancient magic in the ribbon as soon as it appeared. A magic that could lead to a great imbalance if it was not returned to where it belongs. I believe it came to me because I could protect it from the unworthy, if it came to that. Thankfully it has not."

Zey frowned and looked down at his fist as it closed over the ribbon. "But I am not the worthy one."

"You are not the one the Onuei seek, no. But you are worthy of a great many other things Zeymlardterrerd-jormljerra."

She turned her knowing look at me, and I raised my eyebrows, impressed she'd managed to say his long-ass full name correctly and confidently.

"You're Emmaline, part of the Triarchy," I said as her identity clicked into place in my mind. She was part of a reclusive, but very powerful coven. These witches were spoken about in hushed tones among the witch communities. They were members of the House of Spirit and

Sapphire and were called upon to assist in only the most secretive projects. I knew of them and some of the work they'd done for us, but even I had never laid eyes on any of them.

"Have you been in contact with the House of Spirit and Sapphire?" I reflexively took a step forward, angling my body between her and Zey. "Is this a trap?"

Zey gently touched my shoulder as Emmaline smiled.

"This is no trap, I promise," she said. "I have already handed the Onuei over, and you're free to leave anytime."

I wasn't sure I believed her. We were so close to finishing this thing, it would be just my luck that it all went tits-up right at the end.

"Wait a minute." I shook my head, something occurring to me. "Why didn't my power lead us here? When we found the first Onuei, we were much closer to here than to Brazil, which is where the strongest thread led."

"It's because of the protections I placed on it," Emmaline explained. "And the protections of this place. Time and space act a little differently here."

"What does that even mean?" I huffed. "What's your angle here?"

"Sky." Zey's voice was gentle as he dragged his hand down my arm in a soothing touch. "It's OK. She's not showing any signs of being deceitful. I believe her."

"Where's the rest of your coven?" I asked. Why weren't they all here?

At this, Emmaline looked a bit worried, the uncertainty written plainly all over her face. Funnily enough, it was this that made me believe she was being genuine. The girl clearly couldn't hide what she was feeling to save herself.

Emmaline squared her shoulders, visibly trying to stand more confidently as she said, "They don't know . . . it's better if they don't know you were here or that I ever had the Onuei."

"Why?" Keeping something like this from the House of Spirit and Sapphire was not advisable. She'd be treated like I was—a traitor, scum, the enemy.

"It's complicated . . ." Emmaline looked over her shoulder, eyes widening. I followed her gaze, but there was nothing but verdant oasis. She was clearly hearing something we weren't. "You have to go now. If I don't get back soon . . . it won't be good."

"For who? Are you OK?" I took a step closer to her. I was quickly moving from suspicious to worried for this ethereal young woman. She was clearly very powerful, but there was something vulnerable about her at the same time.

"I'll be fine. Please, go now," she rushed out as she waved both hands in a wide arc and opened a portal.

"Holy shit," I muttered, shocked and impressed and a little scared all at the same time. She'd opened a portal. Just like that, with nothing more than a casual wave of the hand. She didn't even chant a spell or require a sacrifice! *Holy shit* she was powerful.

Through the swirling magic, I could see a brick wall. I had no idea where she was sending us, but it wasn't back out into the desert.

I was about to ask where the portal went, demand she tell us if she was in danger, but Zey gripped my hand and pulled it up to rest on his chest.

"No more questions, Sky." He tied the ribbon around my wrist as he spoke. "Let's finish what we started."

I was so floored that he was trusting me to hold one of his precious Onuei that I let him lead me straight through the portal without saying another word.

I turned just in time to see Emmaline with a wide smile, waving at us, as the portal closed.

Raising my wrist, I stared at the delicate ribbon wrapped around it. When I looked up into Zey's eyes, the question must've been evident in my gaze, because he gave me a small, almost sad smile.

"You are worthy," he said simply, pulling me close, his arms around my waist.

"Of what?" I held on to his shoulders, melting into him.

"Everything," he breathed with so much conviction that it took my breath away. Our lips met, our bodies, our souls, coming together like it was the most natural thing in all the realms. Zey was not from this world, but I never felt more like myself, never felt more right than when he was near, holding me, kissing me.

I kissed him with more fervor, holding him tighter.

It was going to hurt like a bitch when I had to let go.

A cold shiver made me break the embrace. Wherever Emmaline had portaled us to was much cooler than the Sahara or even the oasis she'd led us into.

I took in our surroundings, but we were in an alley that could've been anywhere—brick walls on three sides, several dumpsters lined up, the sounds of traffic beyond.

"Sky, there's something—" Zey started to say, but I cut him off by stepping away from him and towards the end of the alleyway. The telltale sound of a dinging tram had drawn my attention.

"She sent us right back to Melbourne," I said, then summoned a warm coat for myself and pulled it on. I smiled, appreciating the powerful witch more and more.

Zey came to stand behind me, his heat radiating into my back, and the smile fell from my lips as I leaned back against him. Having to find our way back to Australia the hard way would've been more dangerous, but it would've given us more time together.

"Sky." Zey sounded serious, my name on his lips heavy and full of something I had a feeling I didn't want to examine too closely. "We should—"

"Figure out where we are and get to the portal." I nodded, avoiding looking at him. Avoiding pain like I always did.

But this time, Zey turned me to face him and made me look at him.

"We should talk," he said. I swallowed, wanting to squirm out of his hold and burrow into his chest all at once. I shut all that shit down and held his gaze.

"What's the point?" I asked, gritting my teeth.

His brow furrowed but it wasn't the pure ire that had been his default state when he first crashed into my life. There was irritation there, but there was also confusion and maybe a bit of sadness.

I was perversely comforted to see that he might be as affected by our looming separation as I, but I knew hearing him voice it would only make it harder for me. For him too. It was better this way.

I took his hand, softening my tone like my heart had softened towards him without permission. "We're so close. Let's finish this."

After a long moment, he pressed his lips together and nodded.

Not wasting any time, I looked around the corner and up and down the street, getting my bearings. We were in the heart of the city—in Spirit and Sapphire territory—the streets bustling with busy people going about their business. We were only a few blocks away from where the portal had opened.

This area would be No Man's Land soon—just like all areas around a portal. It was one of the rare things all Houses agreed on. The damn border of our territory would have to be readjusted again. I wondered whom they'd put in charge of that and almost rethought my determination to get my name cleared and my job back. Hopefully they made Marina do it since she wanted more power so badly.

"There are many Vuulectians in the area," Zey murmured, shifting to his female form as I summoned a hat and tucked my hair under it.

"How many?"

"Dozens. More."

"Are they coming our way?" I was so sick of these bastards. They were multiplying faster than rabbits in breeding season.

"No. I don't believe they're searching for me or the Onuei. They don't expect either to be in this area. Still, we should move quickly."

"Yeah, yeah, what else is new?" I grumbled and took the lead up the street.

Keeping our pace swift but unhurried, I stayed out of people's way and took alleyways where possible. We ducked into a deep stone doorway a few hundred feet away and across the road from the portal. Now that it was common knowledge a new portal had opened, the crumbling ruins of the church it had appeared in had been demolished.

The Portal Guard were crawling all over the area, as well as multiple Vuulectians. They were in their original, faceless forms, no longer trying to hide in plain sight.

"You just need to get to your side of the portal and the Onuei will find your next leader, right?" I asked. We hadn't actually discussed this final step of the plan. I guessed we hadn't wanted to get ahead of ourselves.

"There is a process to releasing them from the inanimate objects, but it is fast," Zey explained.

"Can we release them here? Just, like, shoo them through the portal somehow?" Wishful thinking? Probably.

"I don't know. It's never been done before. But even if I was certain they would go through the portal and not scatter again, there's no way to know if the magical barrier on the other side has been lifted. We can't just release them right into the hands of the Lineg Legion." A muscle in his jaw ticked as he ground his teeth at the mention of those troublemakers.

"Yeah, fuck those guys. OK, so if I can manage to create some kind of distraction and you approach from the other side, maybe . . ." All I had to do was walk up to all those portal guards and announce myself. I was positive all attention would be on me. Then Zey could sneak through the portal, release the Onuei, and leave me forever. Wham, bam, thank you ma'am.

"As soon as you're identified, the Vuulectians will start to seek for me, and they will locate me immediately. I'd never make it through."

I hummed, grudgingly agreeing. "What's the alternative? Because I'm out of ideas."

"We need help."

"In case you haven't been paying attention, everyone thinks we're the bad guys here. We're on our own."

"You've had to do a lot by yourself, Sky, I know that now."

It was a random thing to mention at such a time, and I looked at him, confused. He was watching me with a kind expression.

"But life is not so black-and-white. And you don't have to do everything alone all the time. The Lineg have convinced your people that we are the ones trying to do harm, but surely there are others who can be convinced, reasoned with? If I could just get a message out to my people . . ."

I had no idea how he could have any kind of faith in people—of his world or mine—after all the bullshit we'd had to deal with, but he did give me an idea. I wasn't so sure anyone powerful enough to help us could be reasoned with, but we might have a chance at negotiating.

Pulling him in by the neck, I planted a kiss on his soft lips and gave him a small smile.

"You're a cinnamon roll deep down and your gooey center would be eaten alive here." He frowned, looking confused and kind of horrified. "Now come on, let's go sell our souls to another devil."

"Are you alright, Sky?" He sounded genuinely concerned as he took my hand, but he still followed me without question. "You are referring to me as a baked sweet treat. Are we going back to Celestia? For what purpose?"

I laughed, the feeling bittersweet. I was going to miss his weirdo cluelessness about colloquialisms.

"They're just expressions, Zey."

CHAPTER 20

The House of Air and Amethyst didn't have any territory in Australia, but I knew of a powerful fae who was a member and kept an unofficial residence in No Man's Land west of Melbourne.

I ducked my head and started walking that way.

If the demon Philatanus had seen fit to make a deal with a new species, steal from his own House, and hide it all from everyone, it stood to reason that others could be persuaded to do some less than savory things too. Like helping a couple of fugitives through a portal.

I knew this particular fae had the kind of pull and resources to actually be able to help us—and was self-serving and ambitious enough that he might be willing to try. I just hoped that he was there and that what he wanted in return was more valuable to him than handing us over immediately.

"Where are we going?" Zey asked, wrapping an arm around my shoulders casually, like it was something he did all the time.

"Like you said, we need help, so—"

A massive *boom* ripped through the air, the noise cutting off any other sound. The very ground under our feet shook. Zey and I held on to each other, but the tremor was brief.

People started to scream and yell, the chaotic noises mixing with the sound of glass breaking and heavy things toppling over.

Several winged individuals took to the sky, flying away from where we'd just been. Away from the portal.

Zey and I shared a look and doubled back to look around the corner.

Something had exploded.

The building right next to the portal was decimated. It looked like someone had taken a messy bite out of the top right corner of it. People were streaming out of the front doors, looking terrified. There was debris everywhere, and a few parts of the building were on fire.

A water fae appeared from the opposite side of the street and started putting them out.

The portal guards were helping the injured while others were scanning the area for whom or what had caused this. They were sticking close to the portal—as was their duty—but they weren't all that focused on it.

Even the Vuulectians had backed off several feet, instinctively shrinking away from fire.

"Holy shit." I gripped Zey's wrist, my eyes glued to the scene. "This is either the most wonderful coincidence, or—"

"It's a distraction so we can get to the portal," Zey said. "Doendru is here, she was waiting for me, looking for me when no one else was, and set the explosives off when she felt me nearby. She's urging me to take the opportunity while I can."

"What if it's a trap?"

"It's not." His voice was firm, final.

If he was sure it wasn't a trap, I trusted him. That's how far we'd come. I trusted him without hesitation.

"Then what the hell are we waiting for?" I spun to face him and found him staring at me intently. His depthless eyes had never looked so expressive, so conflicted before.

We didn't have time to talk or have an emotional goodbye. There was no sense in wondering if that look in his eyes was there because he was as torn up about this coming to an end as I was.

As was typical of our time together, we were out of it.

While I untied the ribbon on my wrist, I summoned the one shielding spell I owned. It wasn't as rare as a portal spell, but still expensive and difficult to get into an object for easy use.

I pressed both into his hand and said the incantation. The protective shield enveloped him in warm magic.

He glanced down at himself, then at the Onuei in his hand, confused.

"Sky, no." He shook his head.

"Yes. This will keep you safe from physical and magical attacks for five minutes. Go. *Now!*" I shoved him in the direction of the portal. I wanted to wrap my arms around him and never let go, but I pushed him away instead.

With one last reproachful look over his shoulder, he sprinted towards the portal.

I jogged after him at a much slower pace so I could keep an eye on the whole scene. As I went, I started summoning zaps. There was a stupid amount in the area; it was like picking overripe fruit off a tree—they were practically falling into my hands. I discarded them as I went, leaving them out of reach of anyone who could use them.

About fifty feet from the portal, the Vuulectians realized what was happening, and all hell broke loose. There was no shouting or pointing. They did all their communication telepathically, and they snapped their heads towards Zey and dropped what they were doing.

Suddenly there were dozens of faceless figures rushing at the man I loved.

Fuck. I *loved* him.

I broke into a run, throwing zaps as I went. I'd gotten used to them enough to be able to hit my target nine times out of ten. Vuulectians dropped one after another all around Zey, and I'd gotten at least ten of them before they figured out Zey was shielded.

Any zaps or punches thrown at him bounced right off, but he still couldn't rush through a crowd of bodies trying to stop him.

The portal guards finally realized what was happening and started shouting. It didn't take them nearly as long to spot me.

I shifted my focus to them. Zey had the advantage of the shield, and I'd thinned the herd, so he was able to take the half a dozen or so Vuulectians between him and the portal. He was gaining ground as he fought.

Summoning my trusty blade, I threw it at the nearest guard. It was so familiar, this weapon, like an extension of my body. It hit its mark, embedding itself in the guard's shoulder.

A gun appeared in my grip next, and I opened fire, adding the obnoxiously loud sound of a firing gun to the already chaotic noise all around. I aimed to incapacitate—I didn't actually want to kill anyone. These guys were just doing their job.

Pain exploded in my ribs, and I yelled reflexively. Firing off one more shot, I glanced down to find one of those zaps in my side. The low electric current was making it feel like the pain in my ribs was being delivered to every one of my nerve endings.

"Motherfucker," I grunted as I gripped the handle and yanked it out. I looked up just in time to see a portal guard rushing towards me on my other side. I threw the zap, and it got him in the shoulder, stopping him in his tracks. The same pained expression I'd been wearing moments ago crossed his face.

As he dropped to his knees, I caught sight of the street behind him. There were Vuulectians running towards the portal. Towards Zey. The others must've called for help, and every damn one in the area was probably on their way here.

Eyes wide, I ran. I ducked under the arm of a tall portal guard and kicked him in the knee. The pain in my side was horrible, but I gritted my teeth and kept going.

I saw the exact moment that the shielding spell wore off. We really had run out of time now. If we didn't get those Onuei through the portal *immediately*, it was all over.

There were only two Vuulectians left standing, but one of them landed a punch, finally, right to Zey's jaw. It took both of them by surprise, and he stumbled back. The other one pulled a zap and stabbed him in the back.

Zey yelled out in pain, and I could've sworn I felt it reverberate in my own wound.

They descended on him, searching him for the Onuei. They'd only managed to pry the necklace from his grip when I reached them.

I yanked the zap out of Zey's back and jammed it into the one who'd stabbed him, right where a face should've been.

Zey and I swung for the last Vuulectian standing at the

same time. The force of our combined punches to its gut sent it falling onto its ass, and I snatched the necklace from it just in time.

With an almost painful grip on my wrist, Zey pulled me down as something flew over my head. I didn't even know which direction it had come from.

Injured, tired, and with certain death barreling towards us from every direction, we scrambled to our feet.

I knew, realistically, that all those Vuulectians would follow us through the portal, and it would all be over anyway. But I was determined to cross through that magical barrier. If it was going to end, I was at least glad we'd be doing it together.

Clutching each other, we stumbled the final few steps and jumped sideways into a world I'd never even known existed until Zey appeared in my life.

CHAPTER 21

W e landed in a puddle. At the impact, the wound in my side felt like it was being torn in two, and I cried out.

Zey was up first, probably already healed from all the water around us and the humidity in the air. He picked me up roughly and pulled me away from the portal—away from the chaos.

The puddle we'd landed in wasn't so much a puddle as just a layer of water that stretched out in all directions. There were natural undulations in the landscape, places that were higher than others and looked dry, as well as all kinds of odd-looking plants. Everything other than the dry hills was covered in an inch of water.

In the far distance, I glimpsed something that may have been a city or a settlement—a grouping of building-like shapes. But it was hard to really focus on anything with all that was happening around us.

Water splashed violently in every direction as black shapes blurred in movement, the Vuulectians clashing in battle.

The ones that had been about to descend on us came rushing through the portal only to be immediately met with resistance. I had no idea what was happening, but I had a feeling it had everything to do with the Onuei. The Vuulectians were at war, tearing each other apart already.

There were many more and varied weapons than the zaps here. Some had whips, others crossbow-like weapons, and I had to duck as a spear went sailing over my head. All of them had those electric tips like the zaps. They were the only weapon I was familiar with, so I ignored the rest and tried to summon a zap.

I sighed with relief when one appeared in my hand. I was never certain my ability would work in another realm, but it hadn't failed me yet and wasn't about to start in this new one.

Some of the Vuulectians were clearly on our side, because they rushed over to protect us as Zey pulled the Onuei out of his pockets and laid them out on the ground. But they weren't the only ones who'd noticed our arrival, and they had their hands full.

I threw the zap at one of the Lineg as they took down one of our defenders and rushed for Zey. Pain shot through my side, and I winced, but I hit my mark.

Zey's eyes darted to the prone attacker only a few feet away, then scanned me, zeroing in on my wound.

"Sky. You're hurt." He sounded downright pained and looked genuinely worried.

"I'm OK. It's not that bad," I lied. "You do your Onuei juju, and I'll keep a lookout. Hurry."

If he didn't succeed at his mission, his people looked like they'd destroy each other until there was no one left to lead. And then all of this would've been for nothing. If he didn't save his world, he couldn't help me or himself.

Priorities.

He narrowed his eyes at me but quickly got back to his task.

"You've been extra bossy today," he mumbled as he cradled the window crank in both his hands and held it up above his head.

I chuckled, even though it hurt. He'd been about to say *bitchy*, not *bossy*.

If we actually make it through this, I promised myself, *I'm going to tell him I love him.*

There were no magic words or special ritual. Zey just closed his eyes and held the Onuei, and after a few moments . . . something happened. It was difficult to understand, because there was no glowing, no magical sparks or ethereal sound. But I still felt like I somehow *knew* when the Onuei was released from the inanimate object.

It almost felt like taking a deep breath of the freshest air —the kind that was cleansing and calming and made you feel connected to nature.

Whatever magical barrier had kept it from going to the next True Leader must've been gone—perhaps removed by the warriors fighting to protect us—because I felt it when the Onuei disappeared.

The Vuulectians must've felt it too, probably with far more clarity than I did, because for a split second, they all paused. Everyone in the area stopped and turned their face-less heads in our direction.

Then the fighting started up again, even more fierce.

Zey picked the necklace up next. I summoned another zap and threw it at an attacker. I missed. My wound was making me slow and clumsy. Thankfully, someone on our side took the attacker out before it was too late.

Bodies were starting to pile up in the water all around

us. Some of them roused and stumbled to their feet after a while but many didn't. Were they dead? Or just stunned so badly that it would take them a long time to recover, like the group I'd electrocuted at the dump that night?

I felt that deep breath feeling wash over me again. Another Onuei was released from the object it had been hiding in. That time, the fighting barely stopped.

Zey dropped the necklace and picked up the ribbon.

In a last-ditch effort, the Lineg rallied and rushed us. Our protectors couldn't stop them all. I summoned a zap into each hand and braced myself, shuffling over to block Zey. If I could even buy him a few seconds, it could make all the difference.

I managed to take out two of them—between getting punched in the face and kicked in the knee. But there were too many, and they were desperate, and I was injured.

Two of the Lineg rushed Zey. One of them stabbed him in the neck with a zap, and he went down. The other one snatched the ribbon.

I tried to make myself run after him, push through the pain, but a third Lineg tackled me, and I screamed.

Even through the pain, I could make out what was happening around me.

The fucker with the ribbon was trying to get away, but the good guys weren't making it easy for him and his growing group of fighters.

Everyone was flocking to the ribbon now. Everyone except the asshole on top of me.

It only took a few moments for Zey to come to again— about the same amount of time it took my attacker to pin me to the ground, climb over me, and pull a knife.

Vuulectians had no use for sharp weapons. This one

was armed specifically for me. To hurt me, maybe even kill me.

Zey groaned, his skin doing that flickering ripple thing as he sat up. He looked groggy as he glanced over.

The Lineg had one hand at my throat as the other raised the blade. I was doing my best to thrash him off, but I was so weak. I had a zap in each hand, but he had my arms pinned to my sides with his legs.

Zey whipped his head around, looking in the direction of the retreating fight and the Onuei getting further and further out of his grasp.

He jumped to his feet. He was going to chase after it. He was going to leave me here to die, not willing to let anything jeopardize his mission.

I loved him, and he was going to let me die.

I stopped trying to struggle. There was no fight left in me.

I hoped he'd succeed—restore order to his world and his people. If I had to die, something positive better come out of it.

But also, a part of me hoped he'd have to carry the guilt of my death with him for the rest of his life.

Asshole.

The hand at my neck disappeared a split second before the heavy weight on top of me did too.

I spluttered, trying to get myself upright as I swung the zaps haphazardly.

Warm hands caught my wrists firmly, and I finally realized that Zey was crouched before me. His depthless eyes were wide as they bounced around my face and body. I let the zaps drop from my grip, barely able to hold on to them anyway, and he pulled me into a fierce hug.

"You lied," he admonished, the words sounding choked in his throat. "You're badly hurt."

"You saved me." I sounded nasally, probably from the broken nose. "You chose me."

He pulled back, his hands holding my face as he looked at me fiercely. "I'll always choose you, Sky. I love you."

Despite how fucked everything was, a smile pulled at my lips.

Now I felt bad about thinking he'd left me and calling him an asshole in my mind.

"What about—"

Zey fell back onto his ass, one of those zappy arrows sticking out of his chest.

Eyes wide, I reached for him, but then another hit him in the shoulder, then another and another. I lost track of how many arrows were embedded in him before he fell to his side, water splashing around him.

I pulled myself over to him and yanked out the first arrow I could grab. I only managed the one before pain shot up my back. The bastards had shot me too. I could feel the electric current running through my body, making everything feel like it was on fire.

I collapsed next to Zey, half my face in the shallow water.

He was facing me, and for a moment, I was mesmerized by the blood seeping from my nose and trickling towards his peaceful face.

Forcing my eyes past him, I looked into the distance where the fight for the last Onuei raged on.

I closed my eyes and let my ribbons unspool in my mind's eye. My power was the only thing that still felt strong as my body gave in. The ribbons snapped out and wrapped around what I was looking for.

It was mostly instinct, partly me imposing my will, and partly the very essence of my ability just doing what it was made to do.

With the last dregs of my consciousness, I took a firm grip on the Onuei and *pulled*.

As my magic did my bidding, I managed one last, deep breath before darkness pulled me under.

CHAPTER 22

I came to slowly—not in a shallow pool of water, but in something soft and dry. My eyelids were so heavy, and I managed to lift them barely a sliver on my first few attempts.

I could hear water trickling somewhere nearby, and the fuzzy glimpses I managed through stubbornly lethargic eyelids told me I was somewhere bright.

There were no voices talking around me, no beeps of hospital machines. My mind cleared up enough for me to realize I wasn't dead. Good. That was good.

I thought I was alone, but when I tentatively shifted my body, my left hand stretched out over the soft bedding and there he was. Even with my eyes closed, I knew it was Zey who took my hand in his, his thumb caressing my wrist.

Turning my head to the side, I managed to open my eyes.

"Are you watching me sleep?" My voice was weak and croaky, but he quirked a little smile and I returned it and nothing else mattered. "Creep."

"Oh, you have no idea," he murmured. "I've been

watching you sleep for two days, five hours, and eighteen minutes now."

"Wow. That's a new level of creep. I'm impressed."

We shared another, bigger smile. I was feeling more awake by the second, my mind slowly catching up and processing everything that happened before my epic nap.

"Did they stop that douchebag?" I asked. "Did they release the final Onuei?"

Zey reached up with his free hand, tenderly brushing some matted hair off my cheek. "That's the first thing you're worried about?"

"No. The first thing I worried about was you watching me sleep." I chuckled. He smiled in return, his hand still caressing my cheek, trailing down my neck, my shoulder. "But seriously, we've been single-mindedly on this mission for some time, and I inconveniently passed out before we could see it through. I left myself on a cliff-hanger, so . . . lay it on me. Did we fail?"

"No, we didn't." He was being cagey and slow and affectionate, like it was a casual pillow chat on a Sunday morning. Not like I was asking about the fate of his entire realm.

"Zey, what happened?" I smacked him lightly on the chest and left my hand there, enjoying the feel of him. "I tried to summon it so maybe one of your people would have a chance to release it, but I have no idea if it worked."

"It worked better than anyone could've hoped."

"What does that mean?"

"You summoned it, but not to you—not the ribbon with the Onuei inside it. Sky, you summoned the Onuei right out of the ribbon. You released it."

"I did?" *Holy shit.* Zey nodded, pride shining in those dark eyes. It left a warm, satisfied feeling inside my chest.

"I didn't even know that was possible. I've never summoned anything that wasn't an inanimate object. Wow!" I laughed. "I summoned the shit out of that thing."

Zey grinned, but it fell off his face quickly when I winced. My body was sore and weak, and my injuries sent pain shooting through me when I moved too quickly.

"You need to be careful," Zey reproached, sitting up and fussing with my pillow. "You're still healing."

I glared at him, about to reflexively demand he not tell me what to do, but I relaxed back into the pillows. He was right—I needed to rest.

Now that I was more awake, I took a look around. We were in a massive bed overflowing with pillows and blankets and ridiculously soft sheets. But it was the only thing in the room that was familiar to me, and it stuck out like a sore thumb.

The space was . . . *minimalist* was the best word I could think of to describe it, but even that wasn't quite right. The walls were a soft gray but didn't look solid like walls should —they looked like you'd sink into them if you leaned against them, like a giant piece of memory foam. There were items in the room that I figured were furniture—a table, chairs, a storage shelf—but they were all very sleek. Everything was smooth lines and monotone shades of black and gray, but it didn't feel cold and unwelcoming.

On the opposite wall were holes in various shapes, reminding me of the holes on a monstera leaf, but more irregular. Nothing more than sky was visible beyond.

"Zey, where are we?" I frowned.

"In Vuulectus," he said matter-of-factly. "In a dwelling close to the portal. The occupants were gracious enough to allow us use of their space while you recovered."

Behind him, I caught a glimpse of a side table. It was

overflowing with an obscene number of vials, potions, powders, and even human medical equipment. I was pretty sure the bag hanging on a pole and connected to—I lifted the blanket and followed the clear tube to my arm—to *me* was called an IV drip. There were also items I wasn't familiar with, like glowing spongy boxes. I figured those were Vuulectian things.

"What's happened while I've been having my beauty sleep?" My mind was starting to race, connecting dots and raising questions all at once. "Are your people OK? Does anyone from Earth know what the hell is going on? Where did you get all this vamp saliva?" There were more vials there than I could afford to buy with a month's wages. And I was paid well.

"We can talk later. You need to rest."

"Zey, I need to know what's going on." I tried to cross my arms but had to abandon the motion because of the IV.

"You need to heal." His stubbornness matched mine. Dammit.

"Fine," I huffed and threw the covers back. "If you're not going to tell me anything, then I'll just have to find out for myself."

He gripped my wrist firmly, keeping me in bed. "Fine, you stubborn woman!"

I leaned back with a satisfied smile.

"I'll tell you everything if you eat." He narrowed his eyes, like that was a hard bargain. Who says no to breakfast in bed? Even my stomach was in agreement, growling loudly at the mention of food.

I nodded and Zey got up, moving to a table in the corner. "What would you like?"

"Have you had all this food here the entire time?"

There were piles of food, way more than one person could eat.

"Of course not. You started showing biological signs of coming to about an hour ago, so I sent for food knowing your weak human body needed sustenance to aid the healing process. What would you like?"

I grinned at him. My weirdo.

"Where did all this come from? I thought your kind didn't really need to eat." There was fried chicken, pancakes, fries, chocolate cake, and all kinds of fruit things I couldn't even see properly from my spot on the bed.

"So many questions." Zey shook his head as he picked up a plate and started piling it with bits of everything.

He insisted on feeding me every bite himself, and I decided to indulge him and allow it. As long as he kept talking.

While I ate, he told me about the moments after the battle at the portal. Apparently, after I released the final Onuei and it went on its merry way to the next True Leader, all the fighting stopped. The Vuulectians felt it when it happened, and both sides knew the fight was over. For them, there was no disputing the Onuei. Even though the Lineg Legion had tried to pervert the natural course of how they worked—tried to force them into someone they decided would do a better job than whom the ancient, wise magic chose. *Idiots*.

It turned out that only a small number of the Lineg were knowingly trying to steal the leadership position for their own selfish gain. The rest of them had been lied to. They'd been told that the Lineg were fighting to get the Onuei back to the True Leader—that the others were the ones trying to corrupt their power.

So, when the last Onuei was released, the majority of

Vuulectians on both sides were relieved and felt like they had won. The small group who had killed the previous leader and tried to steal the Onuei had been apprehended and were currently being detained.

The concept of prison was foreign to Vuulectians, the vast majority of issues and disputes being solved with the aid of intuitive learning and logic before it came to violence or malicious actions. I had questions about this, and we went off on a tangent for a while.

Then I asked Zey to get me a piece of that chocolate cake, and we got back on track.

The True Leader had made their way to the capital of Vuulectus as soon as all three Onuei had made their way to them. They were in the process of restoring order and calm to the people of Vuulectus, setting up their advisory council, and getting settled in as a leader.

They were also prioritizing the issue of how to safely have contact with the realms on the other side of the two portals that were now in Vuulectus.

"One of the things they're seeking advice on from other species is how to handle the issue of the Lineg Legion. We haven't had anyone act in such stark defiance of our established, harmonious way of life in living memory," Zey explained. "We want to make sure we handle this in the best way possible, so we're seeking a lot of advice."

"So your people are communicating with my people?" I asked, licking the last of the chocolatey goodness off my lips. I was so full, I couldn't possibly eat another bite, even though everything was beyond delicious. "Do they know I'm here? Are the Houses cooperating?"

"They know—"

"Wait," I cut him off. "Hold that thought. I need to pee."

Zey gently took out my IV and insisted on smearing vamp saliva on the tiny hole in my arm before he tried to carry me to the bathroom. I drew the line there, so he settled for walking with me across the room, holding his arms out like he was spotting me and I was about to attempt a complex gymnastic move for the first time.

The bathroom was similar enough to what I was used to, although it was more . . . organic. The walls were spongy, and water trickled all over the place while strange-looking plants grew out of various corners and up the walls. The "toilet," Zey explained, used every little bit of "waste" to feed those plants, and I hoped my human secretions wouldn't kill them since they were only used to pure Vuulectian waste. How did they pee? Did they just let it leak out of every pore—the same way they absorbed water? Did they even poo?

I kicked Zey out as I took care of business, but he rushed back in as soon as I was finished and lifted me right off the toilet and into something that vaguely resembled a bath. I was about to complain about being manhandled, but then I melted. The "bath" was more like sitting in the softest, cloudy, spongy surface while warm water trickled all around, coming down the walls to fill the tub.

Zey stripped and got in with me, situating himself behind me and pulling me back to rest against his chest. He produced a soft sponge that seemed to lather itself and started bathing me in slow, gentle strokes.

I moaned and leaned my head back against his shoulder.

"This feels like heaven," I murmured. "But it's going to take more than your dick and the best bath I've ever had to distract me from what I want to know."

"I'm not trying to distract you." He chuckled, kissing me on the temple. "I'm just trying to take care of you."

I hummed. I believed him.

"So, the Houses? The mess on Earth?" I prompted.

"The mess has been cleaned up," he stated, and then proceeded to tell me how it was easy to have proper diplomatic talks with the Houses once the True Leader had been revealed and all the Vuulectians were on the same page.

Zey's friend, Doendru, had been instrumental in getting the word out about how the Lineg Legion were trying to deceive everyone. I didn't understand how they'd all been tricked like that when they had this intuitive learning thing, but he explained that it was new territory, reminding me that nothing like that had happened in living memory. They needed some kind of context, some starting point for the intuitive learning to kick in.

Zey wouldn't have been able to use intuitive learning to speak English before he'd come through the portal and heard it. The Vuulectians who had been tricked couldn't use intuitive learning to know they were being lied to if they'd never considered the possibility. All they knew was that the Onuei were missing—a very unsettling and disturbing thing for all—and there was a group telling them Zey had stolen them and was trying to take them for himself. They had no frame of reference for trying to figure out what was actually happening. They never thought to question what they were told because Vuulectians never lied.

It wasn't until Doendru met us in the Sea and Serpentine headquarters and spoke to Zey that the truth was revealed. She immediately set about getting back home and alerting others to get help. That's why we had the distraction of the explosion at the portal and a fighting chance at releasing the Onuei.

She was taking the lead in ironing out all the confusion with the Houses, making sure they understood who the Vuulectians were, how they functioned as a society, what had gone so horribly wrong when Zey came through the portal. She'd ensured that the necklace was returned to Sea and Serpentine and appropriate apologies were made.

"So, they know everything? Am I off the hook?" I turned slightly to ask. He'd washed my whole body, including my hair, but he'd decided my boobs needed extra attention and was focused on lathering them up thoroughly.

"They know the basics," Zey said, keeping his gaze on what his hands were doing. "The True Leader is meeting with representatives from the Houses as we speak. Doendru is under strict instructions to ensure your involvement is explained and there are no repercussions for you."

"Under strict instructions from . . ."

"Me." He flashed me a small smile. "I was planning to attend myself, provide my firsthand account of the events, but I couldn't leave while you were still . . ." he trailed off, looking haunted and tired as his hands dropped from my chest and wrapped loosely around my middle.

For a few moments, we sat there as he held me.

When this had started, all I'd wanted was my old life back. But as I rested in that bath, held so tenderly by a man who'd dropped into my world and flipped it upside down, I realized I really didn't care anymore. Because I loved him, and he loved me, and we were whole and together, and there was nothing I wanted more than to continue to be held by him just like this.

He'd chosen me.

Twisting until I faced him, I pulled him into a kiss. Our lips moved together slowly, tenderly.

"Sky, there is something I must tell you," he whispered against my lips.

I pulled back slightly so I could look at him, and he raised a hand to cover my mouth. I nipped at his palm and chuckled.

"I have tried to have this conversation several times now, and you keep interrupting, but you must remain silent now." He narrowed his eyes.

I rolled mine but kissed his palm and nodded, and he lowered his hand.

"You have a term on Earth which is very similar to a concept we have here in Vuulectus." His grip tightened on my waist, like he was preparing himself to keep me from bolting. "Mate."

My eyebrows shot into my hairline, but the shock melted away quickly. It actually made a lot of sense when I thought about it.

Zey kept speaking before I could say anything. "Here, it's described as the essence of my being merging with the essence of yours—two perfectly matched entities coming together for eternal harmony."

"Soulmates," I whispered and caressed the hair at the nape of his neck.

"Yes." He nodded. "At first, I didn't think this was possible with someone from another realm, but the more time I spent on Earth, the more I learned about the different species finding mates among each other . . . well, it started to make sense. I think that's why the portal opened where it did. The Onuei tore it open to get away, but they placed it where I could find you—where we could find each other, as we were always meant to."

"The universe literally tore a gash in time and space to bring us together?" I kissed him lightly on the lips, and he nodded. "That is so fucking hot," I added, trying to lighten the mood just a little.

He laughed, but I kissed him again, harder.

Our hands caressed, exploring languidly. I felt him grow hard against me and ground my core against it.

He broke the kiss, his hands in my hair, his breath mingling with mine.

"Sky, you're still healing," he protested.

"I'm OK," I whispered against his lips. "I need you."

He was about to protest again, probably demand I go back to bed, but I raised myself slightly and notched his length at my entrance, and his words died in his throat.

We both sighed, holding on to each other as I sank down. I felt full and safe and loved.

Every time Zey and I had fucked during our brief stay with Abraxos, it had been beyond spectacular. I knew now that I'd already been growing feelings for him, but at the time it had been more about the physicality of it—chasing pleasure and distraction.

As we started to move in that bath, our bodies rolling in rhythm, our foreheads touching, I knew this was different. It was raw and sensual. We were connecting not just as bodies seeking pleasure, but as souls seeking connection, hearts beating as one.

We were *making love*.

I'd always scoffed at the expression in the past, but there was no better way to say it. I loved him. He loved me. And I'd never felt so at home in another person's embrace.

We panted and moaned as we made love, the weird water barely splashing around us. It felt more like it was moving with us, supporting and flowing around our bodies as we came together.

There was no talking, no dirty words whispered or curses yelled in ecstasy. It was pure instinct, this joining. We were in such perfect synchronicity, anticipating each other's movements, holding eye contact the entire time.

We chased our pleasure and drew out one another's in equal measure. It was the most beautiful thing I'd ever seen, the way Zey's expression filled with wonder and pure ecstasy, while I felt my own coursing through every cell in my body.

Wave after wave of the most perfect, satisfying, transcendent orgasm of my life washed through me.

When it ended, we held each other as our breathing evened out. Then Zey lifted me out of the water, dried us both off, and carried me to the bed. He crawled in with me and fell asleep before I did. He must've been exhausted.

I knew he didn't need more than a couple of hours of sleep at a time, but he'd been awake for several days, and it was clearly catching up to him.

Full, clean, and sated, I snuggled a little further into him and let myself drift off too.

I woke up alone, stretching, my hands reaching for him but only finding soft sheets.

Blinking my eyes open, I sat up slowly, looking around the room for him.

Shouting drew my attention to the door. Was that what had woken me?

". . . when I say you can!" Zey yelled, but I'd missed the start of what he said.

Another voice spoke, but I couldn't make out the words. Then they started talking over each other, the volume rising. I recognized that voice!

Grinning, I scrambled off the bed and ran for the door. Halfway there, I realized I was stark naked and rushed back to slip on a robe I found at the end of the bed, then ran to the door and opened it.

There were several people hovering around, most of them Vuulectians, but I only knew Zey—in his original, faceless form—and my best friend.

"Lowell!" I threw myself at the big bear shifter, and he picked me clean off the ground in a tight hug.

"Hey, girl." He chuckled, but I didn't miss the edge of relief to his tone.

"She seems perfectly alright and very awake to me." Lowell glared at Zey as he set me down. I turned just in time to see Zey finish shifting into his human, male form.

"I am only trying to make sure she is safely recovering," Zey said, his tone conciliatory, but unapologetic.

Lowell rolled his eyes. "Yeah, yeah, so you keep saying."

"Zey." I took his hand in mine and waited until he stopped glaring at my friend and looked at me. "I'm OK. I promise. I feel so much better already. And you don't have to do that, you know."

He cocked his head to the side. "Do what?"

"Be a jerk," Lowell mumbled, earning him another glare. I whacked him on the arm but otherwise ignored him.

"You don't have to shift out of your true form for me. I love you, whatever form you're in."

"I know." Zey gave me an understanding smile. "I'm not changing myself to be with you—I actually feel more like myself when I'm like this. I feel more like the real me when I'm with you."

All my insides turned into a gooey mess, and I had to clear my throat to keep my tears at bay. Zey planted a gentle kiss on my forehead and Lowell gagged.

The teasing gag helped break the emotional tension, and I chuckled. A few weeks ago, I would've been gagging right along with him and sharing a look of disgust at a display like that.

"I'll go get you more food," Zey said, turning to leave.

"I'm not hungry," I called after him, but he was already gone. Knowing there was no arguing with him when he decided I needed sustenance, I shrugged and showed Lowell into my room.

"So . . . crazy couple of weeks." He bugged his eyes out before sitting at the table and helping himself to some of the mountain of food I hadn't eaten a few hours ago.

"Yeah, you're telling me." I sat opposite him and picked at some of the fruit. Maybe I *could* eat again.

"I'm really glad you're OK, Sky. I was really worried for a while there."

"You and me both." I sighed and we shared a rare, serious look. I popped a grape into my mouth and spoke around it. "Hey, how'd you find me?"

"I've been in and out the whole time you were sleeping off your bender," he teased. "It would've made my life a hell of a lot easier if cell phones worked through portals. But no, I had to scamper back and forth between all the chaos on Earth and making sure your ass wasn't dead."

"I don't follow." We were in Vuulectus, in some random family's home. How did he even know where to find me?

"Your boyfriend is infuriatingly demanding and unreasonable when he sets his mind to something."

"Yeah, trust me, I know." I chuckled, processing having Zey referred to as my boyfriend. We'd only known each other a few weeks, so it was a bit odd. Yet, at the same time, the term seemed too trivial to be applied to the depth of the connection we had.

"Apparently, he flipped his shit when he came to and realized how badly injured you were. He sent dozens of his buddies through the portal with very specific instructions before having you brought to the nearest . . . er . . ." He looked around at the strange walls and organic-looking furniture. "House?"

"Dwelling?" I supplied.

"Abode?"

"Domicile?"

"Anyway." Lowell chuckled. "He had you brought here while his minions rushed back with a bed and every conceivable item, magical and non, for attending to wounds and healing. One of his buddies was sent to find me."

"Really?" Considering the animosity, I found that hard to believe.

"Yep. Said I was the only one he could trust. I guess because I helped you escape at Sea and Serpentine's ball. And probably also because I'm awesome and you told him all about my awesomeness."

"No, that can't be it." I frowned hard at the fruit platter and scratched my head for extra exaggeration. Lowell threw a pastry at me, and it bounced off my cheek.

"Why didn't he just take me back through the portal and have them take care of me on Earth?" I asked.

"He said he couldn't trust anyone. Everything was still chaotic, their True Leader hadn't arrived in the capital yet, and last he knew, you were both still being hunted."

Aww! He was protecting me.

Lowell sighed. "Judging by the sappy look on your face, I'm probably going to regret telling you this, but dude's been out of his mind for days. He refused to leave your side, threatened anyone who came in to treat you with slow and painful death, and was just generally feral about the whole situation. I think he really fucking loves you."

"Awww!" I couldn't hold it in that time.

"You love him too, huh?"

I nodded my head. "He's my mate, Lowell. I never thought I'd even have . . ."

"I'm really happy for you." My best friend gave me a genuine grin and more emotion clogged my throat. What the hell was happening to me? I hardly ever cried.

"How was the meeting with the Houses today?" I managed to get out evenly, changing the subject.

"Good. I wasn't there in person, but word spreads fast when there's something as big as a new portal and a new species to negotiate with. All accounts I've heard so far are positive. Cooperative talks, friendly diplomatic agreements, plans to meet again, *blah blah blah*. Most importantly, you're off the hook. They've already made a statement about your innocence and the confusion."

"Oh. Good." That meant I could go back to my apartment, my work, my life. But how would Zey fit into that?

"That reminds me—Reginald wants to meet with you as soon as you're fully recovered and ready."

"He's going to fire me, isn't he?" I sighed around a smile. The thought wasn't nearly as devastating as it would've been a few weeks ago. "Think they'll let me stay in Spirit and Sapphire?"

But Lowell didn't give me a sympathetic look and a pat on the shoulder. He grinned. "Actually, I think he wants to promote you."

"I'm sorry, what?"

EPILOGUE

I felt naked without my Fairbairn Sykes fighting knife strapped to my thigh, but there was no use for it here, plus it would probably be rude to meet the leader of an entire world while armed.

I smoothed down the silky fabric of my pants, my fingers lingering where the weapon would've sat. I was dressed in black and gray, the colors simple to fit in with my surroundings, the fabric light and luxurious to accommodate the warm, humid atmosphere. And my anxiety sweats.

It was important to me to make a good impression on the True Leader of Vuulectus. So I'd dressed in a way that was reminiscent of their people's appearance, and I'd pulled my hair back into a sleek ponytail. But I drew the line at that. My fuchsia hair had survived being hunted by multiple species across several realms, and I wasn't going to change the thing I loved most about my appearance to please anyone.

Zey took my fidgety hand in his, giving it something else to grip.

I looked up into his eyes and gave him what I hoped was a confident smile.

"You know I can sense your increased heart rate and breathing," he murmured, keeping our conversation private. "I know you're nervous. You don't need to pretend for me."

We were surrounded by Vuulectians and a few representatives from Earth, waiting for the True Leader to join us. The receiving room was Vuulectus's equivalent to a parliament—the seat of power. It was as magnificent as the rest of Zey's home world.

Water trickled everywhere and plants grew right out of the shimmering, smooth floor. Everything was open, and a gentle breeze cooled the space.

"I'm not pretending for you," I whispered back. "I'm pretending for *me*. Fake it till you make it."

Zey gave me a perplexed look. "Lie? To yourself? How? Why? And what are you trying to *make*?"

I laughed, drawing some attention from those nearby. It released some of my nervous tension.

"Colloquialism. I'll explain later." I fiddled with the collar of his already perfectly smooth shirt. I just wanted an excuse to touch him.

There was a hum of energy in the air as everyone turned towards the front of the room, and the few Vuulectians who had been communicating out loud with the others from Earth stopped speaking.

"*The True Leader approaches,*" Zey said in my mind. Yeah, I'd kind of figured that.

This ceremony, one of many meetings and ceremonies to take place that day, was more of a formality than anything. But the past several weeks had been building up to this, and it was hard not to be a little nervous.

I'd met with Reg the day after Lowell told me the high-ranking official of our House wanted to speak with me. Zey tried to insist on keeping me in bed to "rest and heal" for longer, but I'd shut him down. He'd made sure I was pumped so full of vamp saliva and witches' potions and mortal medicine, not to mention food, that I really was feeling almost back to normal.

He'd adorably put his foot down about coming with me —like I'd complain about staying close—and off we went.

The meeting was efficient and smooth. There were apologies about the way we'd both been treated, and Reginald had been quick to offer me the promotion my best friend had mentioned—a directive that had come straight from Odin and Lady Gabriella themselves.

They wanted me to be an ambassador to Vuulectus. All the other Houses agreed—grudgingly, I was sure—that I'd be the best person for the job.

I'd spent a lot of time already learning about Vuulectians and their customs and world, I had an established relationship (professional, of course) with a prominent Vuulectian, and I'd risked my life to ensure the Onuei were recovered and released to the True Leader, thus gaining the respect and trust of their people. Plus—and this part wasn't stated, but I'd worked for a House long enough to know—it was a bonus to Odin and Lady Gabriella that I was a member of the House of Spirit and Sapphire. That would give them a political advantage over the other Houses, and they were eager to lock me in as the ambassador from Earth before the others could find a way to weasel one of their people in instead.

Zey was quick to point out how horribly they'd treated me after years of loyal service, but Reg wasn't bothered. He just offered me as much compensation as I wanted and whatever working conditions I desired.

I took full advantage of my leverage. I was going to be paid an obscene amount to split my time between Earth and Vuulectus, working to ensure a positive, collaborative relationship between the two realms. I'd be spending a lot of time with my Vuulectian counterpart too.

All that was left was for the True Leader to declare that a new position had been created and appoint Zey to said position. Vuulectus had never had need for an ambassador in the past, but now that they had two portals, it was a clear necessity.

Scores of proud, regal Vuulectians came streaming into the room—an impressive feat considering they had no faces to show their proud, regal expressions. After them came the True Leader. Nothing marked this particular figure as different from anyone else in the room except the deep teal cape they wore.

The Leader and their advisors and officials took up spots at the front of the room, and proceedings began.

"After this," Zey said. *"I'd like to take you to see some options for a home around here."*

I smiled at him but didn't dare respond any other way in the silent space. The Leader was speaking out loud—for the benefit of the Earthly visitors, I was sure—but everyone else was dead silent.

Zey and I would be splitting our time between here and Melbourne, so we were house hunting in both areas.

I was hoping to find a place on the river on the Earth side of the portal. Zey would like being so close to water.

THE END

***

If you've enjoyed Sky and Zey's story, it would mean the world to me if you could leave a review on Amazon or Goodreads. Thank you!

If you haven't read *Reject Me, Queen Me, Haunt Me* or *Crave Me* yet, you're missing out! Seriously. You are. (I may be biased, but it's true.)

Ruin Me is due out next month! While I recommend reading in order, they are standalones and can be read out of order, too. Check out the series here: https://www.amazon.com/dp/B09SP11F59

Want to know about future releases without having to follow the authors everywhere? Text "**IMMORTAL**" to **(844) 506-1510**

Note from the Author

Want exclusive access to advanced copies of all my books?
If you're a blogger, bookstagrammer, booktoker, or reviewer,
join my master list and never miss an ARC opportunity!

https://kaydencesnow.com/masterlist

ACKNOWLEDGMENTS

First and foremost, thank you to Kel Carpenter for creating this world and inviting me to play in it. It's been a blast! Thank you to all the other wonderful, talented authors involved in this project. It has been so great getting to know you all and working together.

Massive thanks to my editor on this project - Melinda Andrews. You killed it! My beta readers who have stuck with me from day one - you rock! To all the ARC readers, for your commitment to this world and this series - thank you so much.

Thank you to every single reader who has ever picked up one of my books. I'm living my dream because you're reading my stories.

To Summer - thanks for being SO demanding when you want affection that I'm forced to step away from my desk and take a break.

Thank you to my husband, John. My support, my cheerleader, my partner in every sense of the word. I love you more than you will ever know.

ABOUT THE AUTHOR

Kaydence Snow has lived all over the world but ended up settled in Melbourne, Australia. She lives near the beach with her husband.

She draws inspiration from her own overthinking, sometimes frightening imagination, and everything that makes life interesting: complicated relationships, new experiences and good food and coffee. Life is not worth living without good food and coffee!

She believes sarcasm is the highest form of wit and has the vocabulary of a highly educated, well-read sailor. When she's not writing, thinking about writing, planning when she can write next, or reading other people's writing, she loves to travel and learn new things.

To keep up to date with Kaydence's latest news and releases sign up to her newsletter here:

kaydencesnow.com/#newsletter

Join her reader group here:

facebook.com/groups/KaydenceSnowLodge

Or follow her on: